Hello, Agnieszka!

Between Two Worlds Series, Book 2

EJourney

Sojourner Books
Berkeley, California

Publisher's Note: This is a work of fiction. Names, characters, places, and incidents are a product of the author's imagination. Locales and public names are sometimes used for atmospheric purposes. Any resemblance to actual people, living or dead, or to businesses, companies, events, institutions, or locales is completely coincidental.

Hello, Agnieszka!/EJourney

ISBN-13: 978-0-9962474-2-9

Sojourner Books

Cover Design/Ana Grigoriu/Books-design.com

Line editing and proofreading/Richard Journey, Ph.D.

Book Layout ©2013 BookDesignTemplates.com

Some of us think holding on makes us strong; but sometimes it is letting go.

—HERMANN HESSE

Music is the divine way to tell beautiful, poetic things to the heart.

—PABLO CASALS

Contents: *Hello, Agnieszka!*

1. Secrets

Elise Halverson-Thorpe sat, perusing a client's testimony at her desk in mid-afternoon, green highlighter in hand. She still had a half-inch thick of testimony transcripts to go through before she could stop for the day. She might have to bring some work home again.

She lifted the highlighter to mark a phrase in the transcript, but the cellphone in her shirt pocket vibrated and interrupted her movement for an instant. She groped for the phone while she dragged the clear green ink across the phrase.

She knew it couldn't be Greg, who usually called sometime around noon. Before she swiped it, she glanced at the screen.

"Dad," she muttered to herself, surprised to see her father's face.

He rarely called her at work, aware that she might be arguing a case at court or taking testimony or deposition from a witness. What could he want from her at two in the afternoon?

"Dad. What's up?"

"We're at the hospital, but don't be alarmed. Everything's okay now. It's Peter."

Her father's voice was low and calm, but she detected an edge to it. He was struggling to sound normal and in control.

"Peter?"

She put the green highlighter down, next to a red one, and closed the two-inch thick transcriptions of testimony taken from the woman she was currently defending on a murder charge. Her third such case in as many years of working with the Public Defender.

She leaned against the back of her chair and gripped the telephone tighter. Her father was taking a while to answer, and she grew apprehensive with every second he remained silent.

"Yes. He swallowed a bottle of pills. Mom found him unconscious in the tub. But he's okay now."

"What? What are you saying? He tried to ... kill himself? Peter?"

"Yes."

She thought, gasping, refusing to believe that loaded one-word answer: *No, not possible. Not you, Peter. No. I don't understand.* Her mind went blank for some seconds at the weight of it. She began to breathe a little faster as she struggled against what it meant until she could no longer resist the full force of it. A tangle of thoughts and emotions closed in on her: *Why? What's going on with you? Why choose death over life? No! How could you? How could anyone?*

"Elise, are you all right? Are you still there?" Her father's anxious voice broke through her turmoil.

She swallowed hard to clear her throat. "He did it in your tub?"

"Yes, he came last weekend, said he missed us so much he wanted to stay a week. That was unusual, but we never wondered why. We were just so happy to have him with us for a while. He travels so much in his work, we hardly ever see him."

"The pills, how ...?"

"He must have had them. We don't have any in the house."

Still refusing or unable to believe what her father just told her, Elise was silent again. She could hear her father breathing, echoing her own labored one.

She forced herself to speak again. "But ... he's okay now?"

"Yes. Yes. And he's been seen by a psychologist. How were we to know that he was going to do it? Nothing was different about him."

"That's apparently not unusual," she said weakly, her father's news still weighing on her like a huge unsolvable puzzle. *Peter tried to kill himself. But why?*

Her father said, "How can anyone know then?"

That was, at least, a question to which she might have some answer.

She said, "People serious about suicide don't often say a thing, according to our psychiatric experts. We have defendants who attempt suicide and if they have no history of similar attempts, psychiatrists can't always diagnose them early enough to put them on suicide watch." She had to control the quiver in her voice and she hoped she sounded authoritative enough.

"He was in a good mood."

"We've seen that, too."

"I can't help thinking we went wrong somewhere."

"I don't think it's anything you did."

"He made dinner for us twice this week."

"I didn't think he could cook."

"I don't know why we didn't see it coming."

"None of us might have."

"I thought I knew my children very well."

"I thought I knew Peter well."

"I've never seen Peter so hopeless."

"Neither have I. Nor so desperate that he'd try to end his life."

"He's kind of intense."

"But people say that about me, too." Her voice was finally as calm as she wanted it to sound.

Her father let out a long sigh. "We have so many things we must work out. I still have to call Justin. Mom wants you both to come for dinner tomorrow. Greg, too, of course, and Goyo. Can you make it at three?"

"Yes, of course. How is she?"

"Worse than me, I'm afraid. As if she wants to take the whole burden of guilt on herself. Anyway, talk to her tomorrow."

*****

Greg reached out to put his arm around Elise, but she was not there. He jerked his groggy head up toward the clock on his side table—an hour after midnight. He looked around the dark bedroom. After three years of marriage, groping at that space in the middle of the night could still give him a start and a now-familiar sinking sensation in his gut. To his relief, it was only for an instant.

Five years ago, he had awakened to find Elise gone, leaving him alone on their first wonderful night together. He was left with feelings of misery and desolation he hadn't been able to forget. Two painful years followed when he had to face some hard lessons about himself. Those were behind them now.

He saw her standing against the large window, bathed in the greyish yellow light of a partial moon streaming into the room. His gaze traced her silhouetted figure—from her profile crowned in a luxurious halo of golden hair, along the sinuous line of the throat that sloped gently toward her nipples and curved around her breast, then slid down to her belly, slowly swelling from the life she was nurturing in her womb.

His wife had grown more beautiful in his eyes, as the years went by. Maybe, that was what love did to people.

Elise was sipping water from a bottle, and even in the dark, she looked pensive. She crossed her arms in front of her stomach and bowed her head, strands of hair falling on her cheeks. He didn't see much of her face anymore, but he could imagine her anxiety. She was worried; he knew that. That phone call from her father, shortly before she left the Public Defender's office that afternoon, distressed her deeply.

She had phoned him right after to tell him about Peter. She could not continue her work and decided to take the rest of the afternoon off. He hadn't seen her that upset in the three years they'd been married. He decided to come home early. She needed him.

He'd been shocked at the news. The Halversons seemed to be a well-adjusted, but earnest lot with a few quirks to occasionally surprise those who didn't know them very well.

He watched Elise raise the bottle to her lips and drain it of its contents. She tossed the empty bottle in a trashcan, walked toward the bed, and crawled in. As she lay down, Greg lifted the bed sheet and wrapped it around her. She snuggled into his warm embrace, shivering a little.

"Did I wake you up?"

"No, not really. You were quiet. But I can always sense when you're not in bed with me. That's what wakes me up."

"I do have to get up sometimes, you know. And it gets worse as my stomach gets bigger."

"I can't help it."

Her skin felt cold against his and he rubbed her arms and back gently with his palms.

"You're cold all over. Your arms are almost icy."

"Yes, it was probably stupid to get up without my robe on, but I was hot."

"How long have you been standing there?"

"Not too long. I was burning and my mouth was so dry. I had to get me some water."

He lifted her right hand to his lips and blew on it; he gave the left the same treatment. He tucked both hands inside the sheets, next to his warm chest.

"Aren't you glad we have a little refrigerator in the study?"

"You think of everything."

She planted a quick kiss on his chin.

"I can't remember being that thirsty when I was pregnant with Goyo."

"It's not because you're pregnant. You moan, you know, the whole time, with your mouth slightly open."

He grinned, his eyes twinkling in the near darkness.

"Speak for yourself. I watch you, too. You're worse."

She slapped his bare buttocks playfully. Greg laughed softly and gathered her closer.

"Okay, okay, back to sleep. You'll have a long day tomorrow. When are you going to Mom and Dad's?"

It took him more than a year to feel comfortable calling Elise's father "Dad," who had always been "Charles" to him although he was at least twenty years older. They'd been good friends before they became family.

"Shortly after lunch. She wants us there by three, but I'd like to talk to her before Justin and Dad get there. What time do you think you'll come with Goyo? You don't have to, you know."

"Don't I? But I have to. Peter and I aren't that close, unlike Justin and me, but he's family. Besides, this sounds serious and you may need me. Are you very worried?"

"Not about any danger to Peter right now. He's getting help. But I can't shake this feeling some scary thing is going to happen. Like an emotional tsunami we can't escape."

"That is scary, but you may still be in shock. Give yourself time. Tomorrow night, you'll wonder why you were so worried."

"I hope so." Elise didn't sound convinced.

"You sure you don't want Bob to pick you up at your office and take you? It'll be quicker and he likes driving you around. It's been a while since you've been on that train."

"I rode that train from the East Bay all the time. I don't think anything much has changed."

"You're carrying another precious life in here," he said, caressing her belly.

"Goyo went through the same experience. He survived. Don't be such a worrywart."

She pulled his face down and kissed him.

*****

Elise caught glimpses of modern glass and concrete façades, as her train whizzed by office high-rises in the East Bay, on her way to the peninsula from her office. Three years had not altered that landscape, but to her, it seemed fresh again. Maybe, she was merely seeing it with different eyes.

The last trip she took on that train to her parents' home was shortly before she and Greg got together again. That time, three years ago, she had left Goyo with her mother during a hectic week at the Public Defender's Office, and was taking him back to her apartment on the East Bay. She and Greg now lived with their son a quick ten minutes from her parents so she took a different train. Many times, Bob, Greg's friend and right-hand man, drove her to and from her office.

Two years before that last trip, she had taken the same train. Alone, sad, and hopeless, she had given up on seeing Greg, ever again. She'd been pregnant then, as well, and she was going to tell her parents she had decided to have a child out of wedlock. They had been upset, worried that her career would be derailed. Still, they professed faith in her, and offered her help so she could get her degree.

Elise closed her eyes and settled comfortably on her seat. This afternoon, she could pass for a housewife. Granted, she admitted with an amused smile, a housewife in a dark blue suit, getting tight around the stomach. She would have to buy a few maternity suits.

Little Gregory was four now, a frisky little boy who worshipped Bob and Alicia's oldest son, about ten years older than him. Andres, "Andy," who was patient and always indulged the little boy's whims, was the one who christened him "Goyo," a Spanish diminutive for Gregorio. It had stuck because little Gregory could say it and Bob's two boys used it with obvious affection.

At the train station, Elise was surprised to find her mother hovering in the lobby. In the past, she used to wait in her car at the short-term lot for people picking up or dropping off passengers. Her pacing in the lobby could only mean one thing. She was too restless to sit alone in her car.

Her mother smiled at her, but Elise saw deep anxiety in her eyes. Close up, she noted dark shadows that emphasized tiny lines on the corners of her eyes. Furrows on her brow seemed longer and deeper.

What a contrast from the last time she had seen her less than a month ago, at her mother's last dinner party. That time, her sea blue eyes shone, her delicate, sweet face glowed, and nothing but harsh light could reveal shallow lines on her forehead or a slight sagging on her cheeks.

Elise embraced her mother tight.

"How are you, Mom?"

Mrs. Halverson held Elise close and didn't answer.

"You okay?"

She merely nodded her head and, with a hand on her daughter's elbow, led her toward the car.

"Let's go to Peet's. I can't go home yet. We've got more than an hour before your brother and your dad get here. Is Greg coming?"

"Yes, he'll be here with Goyo, maybe sometime after five."

"You're not showing yet."

"No? But I'm going on four months. I can't button my jacket anymore."

"I'm glad you decided to have another kid. I thought you were going to stop at one. You're warm and loving, Elise, a good mother."

Elise was touched at the unexpected compliment. She smiled and kissed her mother's cheek.

"Greg's already talking about a third. He says he knows how lonely it is to be an only child. After that, he'll go for a vasectomy. So, maybe, we'll follow this one with another in two years."

The coffee shop was nearly full but relatively quiet. As usual, most customers sat alone, pounding on computers or squinting at books or hand-held tablets, oblivious to what was going on around them. Elise and Mrs. Halverson made their way toward a small empty table.

"Wait here for me, Mom. I'll get me a latte. Café mocha for you, as usual?"

Her mother nodded. "Remember the whipped cream."

Elise returned, holding one paper cup of coffee in each hand. She handed her mother a cup and sat across the table from her.

The barely two feet of space between them acted like a barrier as they sipped their coffee in silence. Elise regarded the tension and misery on her mother's face, and blinked away the moisture that began to gather in her eyes.

Her mother seemed lost in an inner world that no one could penetrate. Elise wondered how one began to talk about a loved one's attempted suicide, particularly of a brother one adored, and to a mother who had built a wall around her to protect herself from the pain of it.

How could she possibly add to her suffering by talking about Peter now? What her mother needed was some respite. Elise averted her eyes down to the dark brew in her hand.

Peter was not garrulous, like Justin. He was often quiet, but in such a serene, reassuring way that she and

Justin felt they could safely share their secrets with him. He was also active and athletic, but was most earnest about basketball, usually beating Justin at it, although he was shorter than Justin by five inches. As serene as he was, he radiated life, and never betrayed any signs he was depressed.

Minutes later, Elise swallowed the last drop of coffee and glanced at her wristwatch.

"It's a quarter of, Mom. Time to go. I'll drive."

She drove in silence for some time before her mother spoke again.

"There was something more than depression in Peter's suicide attempt."

"I don't understand."

"Oh Elise, your brother is sick, seriously sick."

"Depression can be a sickness. But we all feel down sometimes. Peter tried to commit suicide; so something deeper is going on with him."

"No, I mean, he's really sick. Not just in his mind." Her mother covered her face and burst into tears.

Elise was dumbfounded. Had she not heard the worst yet? She freed one hand from the steering wheel and stroked her mother's back. That was all she could do, for now. They should soon be at her parents' house.

She let out a long breath when she spotted the stuccoed California bungalow where she grew up. She slowed down, steered onto the driveway, and parked next to her father's car.

"Mom, we're here. Dad's already home."

Mrs. Halverson pulled some tissues from a box in the glove compartment. She wiped the tearstains off her face and inspected it in the rear view mirror. She composed herself, opened the car door, and wearily eased her body out of the car.

Dr. Halverson had opened the door by the time she reached it. Elise walked a few paces behind her mother.

Mrs. Halverson gave her husband a slight nod and was about to walk past him, but he caught her hand and squeezed it before she could go in. The gesture was quick and unobtrusive, but Elise sensed the implicit support it conveyed.

"Dad." Elise hugged her father.

He nodded and touched cold lips to her cheek. He put an arm around her shoulders, and led her into the house.

Her mother had gone straight to the kitchen. Elise followed her there. She had already filled a kettle with water, placed it on the burner, and was spooning herbal tealeaves into an infuser. A plate of finger sandwiches covered with plastic rested on the table. She had obviously prepared it earlier that day.

Food and cooking were her mother's way of coping with anxieties. To soothe nerves, she swore by the powers of tisane and prepared it as if it was a ritual. Before her husband came home from his work as economics professor at the university, she would sit sipping tisane in a meditative mood, in front of her butcher-block table.

"Mom, let me help you."

"No, sit down. I need to be busy. Better yet, go talk to your father."

Elise hesitated and stayed where she was. She watched her mother's movements for some minutes. They were efficient, as usual, but she saw a certain desperation in them. Was she merely imagining it because she knew the chaotic emotions her mother was going through?

She envied her mother her rituals. She, herself, didn't have anything like them. Yet, now, she wondered if they were enough to sustain someone who never had to deal with disasters worse than burnt roasts, or an emotional crisis like the one she suffered after she left Greg on their first night together.

Her mother flashed her another glance.

"Go! I'm almost done here."

With one last worried look, Elise left to search for her father. She found him in the living room, his legs crossed, and an arm across his stomach supporting the other arm. His fingers covered his mouth and he had that faraway look and inscrutable darkness in his eyes whenever he mulled over serious problems.

She sat across from him, but he ignored her presence and continued to stare into space. How could she violate that obvious need to be alone? Her father didn't have the busy rituals her mother fell back on in times of tension and turmoil. He was like her. He brooded long hours over whatever troubled him.

She retreated into her own thoughts, summoning pleasant memories of growing up with Peter, and hoping for such happy times again. But her hopes didn't ring true, dashed by the gravity of her mother's grief and the remoteness her father assumed in the face of a tragedy none of them ever expected.

She heard the front door being unlocked, and bounded from her chair. That had to be Justin, she thought with some relief. Her brother had a knack for brightening up the atmosphere, a gift they could use at the moment.

By the time Elise reached the vestibule, Justin was closing the door, his back to her. He smiled when he saw her and approached with open arms to hug and kiss her. But Elise noted something different about him. His smile was forced and she missed the mischievous glitter in his eyes.

Ten minutes later, the family was in the living room having tea. Justin had hugged and kissed his parents and, then, lapsed into silence. Elise thought it was so unlike him and it made her uneasy; but how else was he supposed to act, considering recent events? She and her dad took refuge in silence, so why couldn't he?

Mrs. Halverson sat on the sofa next to her husband, across from their children. They all avoided each other's gaze as they sipped tea. No one, not even Justin who gobbled up everything their mother prepared, touched the finger sandwiches.

Evasiveness, Elise thought, had been rare among the Halversons. Frankness was valued, although never at the expense of someone's misery. Discomfort was endured, if that brought problems or disagreement out in the open. Theirs had been a lively family who hashed out their differences through talking, often until they were hoarse in their efforts to reach resolution. But that was before Peter's attempted suicide.

Silence, she was now finding out, was a safe though uneasy haven at times like these—when great pain was so new, you couldn't contain it; or some fateful truth hidden for so long had to be disclosed; or your reaction was so personal, you couldn't sympathize with another. All those were now true for them.

Elise was certain her mother held in her heart and her mind some secrets that weighed on her. She couldn't even guess what those were, but her mother needed to tell them soon for her own peace of mind. She peered expectantly at her father, hoping to get some help from him.

He met her gaze, with the ghost of a hesitant, helpless smile, but he turned toward his wife, who seemed determined not to look at him. Forehead creased with worry, he watched her for some time while she continued to sip her tea as if it was critical for her to do so.

Elise realized, then, that her father was leaving it to her mother to explain the distressing events of the past week. She could sense his discomfort. *He knows what Mom is about to disclose. Of course, he does,* she told herself. *This family has no secrets.*

For an instant, she glared in annoyance at her father. *Why can't he help ease Mom's misery by taking the burden away from her? He, himself, can tell me and Justin what's going on.* She was about to insist that her father do the explaining when Justin spoke.

"Would you like me to stay for a few days? Help along? Peter and I used to share secrets, tell each other our fears when we were kids. Maybe, he'll want to talk, and I could be there to listen to him."

They were the first words he uttered that afternoon. His voice was steady enough when he began, but he seemed to lose control of it with his last words. He clamped his mouth shut.

Neither parent answered and long minutes went by before Mrs. Halverson raised her face. She had a resolute expression in her eyes and pursed lips.

"Peter is sick. But as I told Elise earlier today, it's not so much in his mind. He has this terrible disease."

Her mother's voice trembled and Elise held her breath. The next instant, she heard her shaky voice splinter into words that seemed to break her heart.

"Peter ... has ... Huntington's disease."

Elise and Justin exchanged bewildered glances, searching their minds for something to help those words make sense. Neither knew exactly what the disease was nor how bad it could get, but they both guessed that it was inherited and quite serious.

At first, Elise resisted the idea of Peter's sickness. The threat of it made her stomach turn and she took comfort in thinking that it was also vague, even surreal. But disbelief could not last. Lifelong habits confronting problems head on prevailed.

As reality sank in, Elise shivered at the cold coursing down her spine. Her first thought was for her son and the child in her womb.

"Are my children at risk? Do we need to be tested?" Her voice was unsteady and her eyes dark with anxiety.

"That's inherited. Who ...?" Justin said, shuddering.

"No, you're both safe," Dr. Halverson hastened to answer.

"But how can you say that, if we haven't been tested?" Elise's voice was shrill as she struggled with emotions she still could not contain.

"Because your father and I were and we don't have the disease. It's directly transmitted," her mother said.

"Then, how ... ?" Justin said, staring at his parents, then at his sister.

Elise knew he was searching for resemblances. She owed her mother her coloring and the shape of her face and mouth but, like Justin, she had inherited her father's large eyes, giving the three of them that wide-eyed look of eternal curiosity. Peter had dark, deep-set eyes under bushy brows.

"Peter is not Dad's." Quietly, Elise completed the thought she sensed Justin was reluctant to give voice to.

Mrs. Halverson peered into her children's eyes. She was pleading, Elise thought. But for what? For understanding? Forgiveness? Possibly even relief from despair and ... guilt? Elise felt even more unsettled. Was there guilt in her mother's eyes?

"Peter is my son, but not ... ." She glanced sideways at her husband and bowed her head. She clasped her hands tight on her lap, her body rigid with tension.

Wordless moments passed as Elise and Justin, both coping with confusing emotions, regarded their mother with concern.

Elise could hear her heart thumping and, before long, she was sure that if she kept listening to it, she would get even more anxious. The silence became too much for her to bear. She and her brother needed more answers.

"Does Peter know that the disease didn't come from either of you?"

"No, not before the doctor told us the test results. The first symptoms are sometimes in the mind ... the attempted suicide." Her mother's words trailed off into trembling silence.

"The doctor at the hospital noticed some physical symptoms, so he ordered tests," she added, after a long pause.

Justin said, "Was there a prognosis?"

"Nothing specific. What we should expect. Peter's father died from the disease more than ten years ago."

She bowed her head again and lapsed into another long painful pause.

After a while, she said, "There's no cure and it keeps getting worse. My son ...."

This time, she turned toward her husband and buried her face on his shoulder to muffle her tears. They were profuse tears. To Elise, they seemed full of anger—probably at fate for what it had dealt Peter and even at herself for being helpless against fate. She and

Justin could do nothing but watch and wait for her to
calm down.

The allusion to another man neither Justin nor
Elise knew—a father to a brother they both adored—
caught them by surprise. Never in a hundred years,
Elise thought, would she have suspected that Peter had
a different father. She was neither angry nor resentful
that it was kept secret. But why the need to keep it
hidden? Her parents knew she and Justin would have
accepted Peter, no matter what.

"Did Peter know about his father?" Elise asked
after her mother stopped crying and had been silent for
some minutes.

"Not before he was diagnosed. We never told
anyone. Peter was born, knowing your dad as his
father."

"True, Dad and Peter are like peas from the same
pod. Nearly the same color hair, similar lean physiques,
although Peter's some inches shorter."

"And they have the same mannerisms," her mother
added. "But people have remarked that Peter didn't
have blue eyes like the rest of us."

"Genetic variations. That's natural."

"That's what your Dad always said. Anyway, to
him, Peter has always been his son."

She grasped her husband's hand and tried to smile
at him. She rose from the sofa and before anyone could
protest, she snatched the teapot from the table.

"I should get us more tea."

Elise swiped at the tears welling in her eyes as she
gazed at her mother's back until she disappeared into

the kitchen. Even in anguish, her mother always thought about their welfare first. More than once, Elise had wondered if such selflessness took something out of her. *How often has she suppressed her own needs, her own desires for her family's sake?*

Elise realized she didn't know this woman as well as she should, beyond her exceptional piano playing and her traditional role as mother—certainly as caring and comforting as her children could hope for. She winced with a twinge of guilt as she admitted to herself that she found her dull, maybe because she limited her interests to her family.

She now understood why her father left it to his wife to disclose the truth. That truth was buried in her mother's past, and had really not been kept secret. Her parents merely allowed it to languish because it hadn't mattered to them. They had assumed nothing bad could happen to anyone in the family. Were it not for Peter's attempted suicide and his threatening disease, they might never have supposed they had "secrets" they needed to share with their children.

Elise understood why her mother seemed reluctant to recount her past. She had been complacent in the tranquil, ordered world her husband offered her. He exuded the same calm reassurance Peter did. But the last tragic week turned her world inside out, and she had to reveal the truth. Though the worst disclosure was probably over, she dreaded having to bare her soul to her children.

II. Family

Elise paced around the living room. She glanced at the clock on a side table every time she passed by it. Her muscles were taut from the tension of the last few hours and she found it impossible to sit still.

Her mother returned to the living room with a fresh pot of herbal tea. She poured the light green brew into fresh cups and handed the first to her husband.

"Maybe, we should have some dinner first. It's early, but I can put something light together in half an hour. Greg and Goyo should be here by then."

"Oh, Mom, we ...." Elise stopped in midsentence when she heard the familiar hum of a car engine. "That's Greg," she said in relief.

She strode briskly toward the vestibule and was out the front door as Greg was turning off the engine.

In the back of the car, Goyo was shouting something she couldn't hear and waving his arms at her. She opened the door on the passenger side and released her son from his car seat.

"Mommy, Mommy!" Goyo jumped into his mother's embrace and wound his arms around her neck.

Elise planted kisses all over his head and cheeks. "Hmmm. You smell of sun and dust, my lively little boy. What have you been doing?"

Goyo looked up at his mother, and his grayish blue eyes, so much like Greg's, twinkled with pride.

"I went jogging with Daddy, and me and Joe, we flew a kite. Andy taught us."

"Oh! Did you and Daddy go out together today?"

Goyo nodded his head several times and snuggled, with a broad smile, against his mother's bosom. Elise knew he waited eagerly for weekends when his father took him on his almost daily run in the afternoon. Goyo, on his bicycle, pedaled alongside Greg who adjusted his pace to his son's speed and paused to let Goyo rest every few minutes. On their first day out together, they were gone for nearly two hours.

"Where did you go fly your kite?"

"Out there. With other guys. They had bigger kites. But ours went up higher."

Greg had descended from the car and walked to the back of it. He said, "Alicia told me he was out at the park with her boys all afternoon."

Greg pulled Goyo's backpack from the trunk and slung it on one arm. He kissed Elise on the lips and peered into her eyes. A frown crossed his brow.

"Has it been that bad?"

"It's been pretty intense."

"Is Peter worse?"

"No, he's better. He's coming home this Friday. But we've had a shock. My normal, picture-perfect family has its lurking secrets, after all. Justin and I were totally not ready for them."

Her words trailed into a murmur. From the sides of her eyes, she had glimpsed her father standing on the front porch, his shoulders weighed down by a hunch new to him. Sadly, she wondered how weighty a burden those shoulders now endured.

Dr. Halverson opened his arms to welcome Greg and Goyo, the corners of his mouth curved up in a smile that belied eyes clouded with anxiety. He greeted Greg with a nod and an affectionate touch on his arm. Greg embraced his father-in-law.

Neither spoke but, to Elise, the connection between the two was as palpable as it had always been. Theirs was a meeting of minds, obvious from the beginning when Greg hired her father as a consultant on business economics. Since then, a deep friendship had grown between them.

"Is my Goyo here to hug me and cheer me up?"

Her father directed eyes crinkled into a smile at his grandson.

Goyo lifted his head, turned, and broke into a broad glowing grin at his grandfather. Dr. Halverson's compressed lips widened with pleasure. Elise inwardly gave thanks that mischievous little boys could sometimes assume the guise of little angels.

Her father gathered Goyo out of her arms and into his own.

"I've missed my Goyo. You always seem bigger every time I see you."

He nudged his nose against the little boy's cheeks.

"You tickle me, grampa."

Goyo wiggled his head around before he hugged his grandfather and kissed him on both cheeks. He wormed out of the encircling arms that supported him, and slithered his body to the ground.

"I'll walk. You don't have to carry me anymore, grampa."

"Okay, but give me your hand and let's go in together. I want to hear what you've been up to."

"I flew a kite today. I told Mommy, but there's more I gotta tell her." Goyo pulled his hand from his grandfather's, ran back to his mother, and grasped her hand.

Mrs. Halverson stood in the foyer, a few paces away.

"Come in, come in. It's warmer in here."

She gave Greg a brief tight hug and mumbled, "Good to see you, Greg. I'm so glad you came. Can I get you something?"

"Thank you, but please don't bother. I'm family now; remember? I help myself freely to the contents of your refrigerator and everything on the dining table."

Greg smiled, an amused gleam in his eyes. He kissed her on both cheeks. Her lips twitched into a smile, but her attention was already on the three who were entering the house. She approached Goyo with outstretched arms.

"I know you've grown too big to be carried but can I lift you up in my arms for a hug and big kisses? That's easier for me. I can't bend down on the floor, anymore."

Goyo nodded and flashed his grandmother a bright smile. But he lowered his head as if in shame, when she picked him up.

"We'll let them bond by themselves," Greg said, as he grasped Elise's elbow and led her into the dining room.

Together, the older Halversons carried their grandson into the living room as they showered him with kisses. They settled on the sofa, the grandparents flanking Goyo. The boy had plenty to tell. They had not seen each other for nearly a month and his grandparents were ready to hang on to his every word and allow themselves to be entertained. He began by recounting his first experience flying a kite.

*****

Greg had spotted Justin sitting by the dining table, watching everyone through the vestibule. Justin nodded a greeting at him and Elise.

He gave Justin a quick hug. He and his brother-in-law shared a droll sense of humor and keen interests in technology and business. They had an easy, bantering friendship, the kind formed between brothers who did most things together in childhood. That evening, Greg saw deep worry on Justin's often-animated face.

"Good to see you, Justin."

"Greg. How's it going? Sis treating you right?"

Greg missed the undertone of mischief he had come to expect from Justin.

"Can't you tell? She's giving me another heir."

He pulled a chair out for Elise and took a seat next to her. Justin glanced at her sister's belly and grinned. For a second, his eyes shone with the impish sparkle that seemed natural to him.

"Heirs are good. What else would you do with your money, bro?"

Greg chuckled, ready for an equally teasing retort, but laughter escaping from the lips of the older Halversons, a few paces away, interrupted him. He craned his neck toward the living room.

The laughter was not the crisp spontaneous duet of roars and trills he had heard from such interactions in the past; but it passed for laughter. He glanced at Elise and Justin, who were also smiling and enjoying the momentary respite from the strain of the last hour. Greg sat back on his chair. He anticipated a long, maybe even distressing night. But for now, he was content, along with his wife and her brother, to listen to his son charm his grandparents.

Sometime later, Elise placed a hand on his arm, her smile still lingering in her eyes.

"Something to drink, sweetheart?"

"No, my love, I'm okay."

"Not even Mom's tisane?"

Greg grinned. "I'm not at that stage yet. And don't worry about Goyo. Alicia gave him a big snack before we left home."

He grasped Elise's hand and squeezed it gently. His gaze shifted from his wife to Justin and back.

"So, you two have had a shock."

"We just learned Peter is not my Dad's son."

Justin's words tumbled out in a flat tone, as if they stated some curious but indifferent fact, like the statistics he was fond of citing.

"Oh." Greg was flabbergasted. No wonder brother and sister looked dazed. Justin's disclosure was like a shot in the dark. He never would have guessed Peter was not Dr. Halverson's son, despite a few obvious physical differences.

Apparently, there was more, and in the same tone, Justin said Peter was ill with an incurable, debilitating, inherited disease. That disease forced their mother to disclose that Peter had a different biological father.

For a few minutes, Greg was speechless. What did anyone say to such a surprising, devastating litany?

"I'm so sorry about Peter."

His words of sympathy sounded hollow, but he thought anything would, in the face of such a tragedy. Silence—the kind conveyed with understanding and empathy—was what the family needed. He remembered Elise's remark about "lurking secrets, and he squeezed her hand in sympathy.

"Mom has more to say, but she seems to be putting off talking to us," she said.

"She's getting her courage up to do it," Justin remarked.

"Maybe. But she should get on with it. She needs to talk, more for herself really than for us. She's feeling guilty and talking would help her purge herself of that guilt."

"Guilt? I don't get it. This isn't her fault. Let's say she was married before or had a boyfriend who got her pregnant and left her. So what? She should know we wouldn't hold that against her."

"No, we know we won't. But Mom has a moralistic streak when it comes to her own actions. We never talk about it, but we all have heard that her parents lived by rigid rules."

"You're right. I do remember that. She's harder on herself than on any of us."

*****

In the living room, an hour later, Elise leaned against Greg on the couch as she sipped a bottle of sparkling water. He pulled her closer and rested his arm on her shoulder. Her gaze wandered around the family seated in front of her.

Justin sat cross-legged on a chair across from them, wine glass in one hand and in the other, a bottle he raised toward Greg. Greg nodded and Justin poured them both their second glasses of red wine.

Dr. Halverson sat on a chair to Justin's left, a half-empty bottle of beer in one hand. On his lap, he held Goyo who was amusing himself drawing on a tablet. For a while, Goyo's chatter was the only sound that broke through their uneasy silence.

Mrs. Halverson shared the sofa with Elise and Greg. She leaned forward in a rigid stance that isolated her, nibbling on a ham and cheese sandwich Elise made for her.

"It can't be that bad." Elise teased her mother with a smile.

"What? What can't be that bad?"

"The sandwich. I can mess up your tagine recipe but Greg swears I make great ham and cheese sandwiches."

Her mother gave the faintest smile.

"No, Not bad at all. It's a good remoulade. You've learned to make it well. It's tangy enough, with a hint of sweetness that goes well with the salty ham. I'm just not that hungry."

"Okay, you're forcing me to reverse roles. You must eat your sandwich and I insist you finish it, to show me you do like it. You used to say that to me when I was balky."

The faint smile broadened and almost touched Mrs. Halverson's eyes. She took bigger bites of her sandwich.

Elise kept an eye on her mother as she ate. Not long after, Mrs. Halverson swallowed the last bite and smiled triumphantly at her daughter.

"There, done!"

"Thank you, Mom, for humoring me."

Elise regarded her mother, trying to fathom her mind, wondering if she was ready to talk. Soon, someone had to say something to prod her to begin her story. She glanced at her brother and her father; both avoided her eyes. She had no choice.

"Now, Mom, I want to hear your story. We all do."

Justin chimed in then. Maybe like her, he was mulling over how to nudge their mother into talking.

"Yeah, Mom. Tell us about you. I've waited a long time. When I was seven or eight, I used to watch you sitting at your butcher-block table, deep in thought. I'd wonder what was going on in your mind; if you had an imaginary world, like I did. But I was a child, self-centered, and sure that the world revolved around me. So, I used to walk away, without saying anything. But, when I got older, I wished I'd asked. After that, we all became too busy."

Elise said, "There's something that bothers me, too. You're so caring and warm. I can't imagine what you could have done that your mother could never forgive you for. What could prompt parents to put such a wedge between them and an only daughter?"

With her fingertips, Mrs. Halverson dabbed the corners of her eyes, moistening again with tears.

"My parents cut me off so young. Why? I may not really understand, ever. I'm sure I was also at fault. I went through hardships and heartache that I swore my children would never suffer from. And, yet, here I am. It's my very own wish to spare you those heartaches that's brought you pain."

Mrs. Halverson scanned the faces of her family, their eyes focused on her. Yes, they had waited a long time for her to tell her story. But, where should she begin? Maybe, nearly fifty years earlier, when she was eight? It was one of her clearest memories of childhood.

III. Agnieszka's Roots

The Past …

"Agnieszka …."

The footsteps grew louder. I lay on my side and hugged my knees closer to make myself as small as I could, underneath the bed. I shut my eyes. If I didn't see her and I stayed still, maybe she wouldn't see me.

"Agnieszka!" The footsteps stopped. My mother was probably standing somewhere next to the bed, but I didn't dare open my eyes or move a muscle.

"Agnieszka, come on out from under the bed. I know you're down there. You can't get away, you know, from taking your cod liver oil or you'll have to go to school without your breakfast."

I had never won against my mother on the battle of the cod liver oil. But she had never denied me breakfast. She had used this threat before but never followed up on it. I was sure I would still go to school this morning with my belly full.

What I really dreaded was the evening when my father was home from work. I could picture what used to happen then, as if it was today. He would hold my mouth open while my mother forced the foul liquid into my mouth. By then, I had gone through this ordeal several times, after I refused to take the oil in the morning.

It was probably easier to obey. I had done it so often before: Pinch my nose, open my mouth, swallow the oil, and gulp a glass of orange juice to wash the oil and its smell all the way down. Then, I would brush my teeth with lots of toothpaste.

But I turned eight a month ago and I was sick of the thing being forced on me. Sick of its smell. Sick of its taste. I'd been made to take the fishy liquid every day as far back as I could remember. By now, that would be several hundred tablespoons. Did it really matter if I skipped a day or two? I asked my mother once to let me skip.

She didn't, but she was as sweet about it as she could be.

"Things which are good for you hardly ever taste good or feel good. But you have to take them regularly. You know I'm making sure you're healthy. We can't afford to get sick. Tata and I take it, too."

So, I lay there, holding my breath, my eyes still closed, aware that asking didn't help. I was thinking of another strategy when I felt a strong hand grab my foot and I was being dragged out from under the bed.

In the kitchen where Mama stored this offensive stuff, I clamped my mouth shut to the tablespoon of cod liver oil in front of my face. She waited. We stared at each other. Minutes seemed to tick by. But it probably didn't take too long before she threw the spoon and the oil into the sink. In the past, she used to take the oil herself.

She scowled, irritated and displeased. She grabbed my arm, my lunch bag and school bag, and shoved me out the door to the porch. At the top of the stairs that led outside, she handed me my bag and my lunch.

"I'm disappointed in you Agnieszka. Go to school. You don't get your breakfast this morning."

On the way to school, I peeked into my lunch bag. I was hungry. I could leave my orange for lunch and have it with the carton of milk the school gave out to pupils. So, I ate my sandwich. When I returned home that afternoon, I was shaking from hunger.

That night, halfway through dessert, my mother got up. A minute later, she stood before me with a tablespoon and the bottle of cod liver oil. Any hope I had that I could escape that day's dose died before I took my last bite of custard.

I swallowed the cod liver oil without protest. My mother hugged me and called me a "good girl." I pushed her away and ran to my room.

*****

I don't want to give an unfair impression of my parents. They were good-hearted working class folks who never left the city they lived in. They came from Poland as children in the mid-thirties and had known about each other for a long time. Their families were neighbors in a community of Polish immigrants in Pennsylvania, and their parents worked in the coalmines. But they didn't actually get acquainted until they were adults.

My parents were shy, solitary people who married
more for convenience than for love. She was twenty-
nine and he, thirty-seven. Several months after they
met, they decided growing older would be easier if they
were together. They never expected to have children,
but three years later, I was born.

My father liked me to call him Tata, not Dad. It
kept him more connected to his "homeland." My name,
Agnieszka, came from the same connection.

Tata worked at Gimbel's as a tailor who did
alterations at the men's clothing department. Mama
was a housewife who took in some sewing.

My parents were Catholic, like most Polish
immigrants. Their religion shaped their experience
growing up in this country. Years later, I understood
how and why from a story Aunt Jola related to me.

Despite the struggle with the cod liver oil, my first
eight years had been normal, uneventful, and happy
enough. My parents didn't loom large when I used to
recall those years. They were not particularly warm or
demonstrative, but they were always there, attending
to each other's needs as well as mine, in their simple,
straightforward ways. I never saw them quarrel or
heard them argue. They had fondness for each other,
but not passion. They spent time with each other only
at breakfast and in the evening, an arrangement that
suited them both.

My most vivid memory of those first eight years
was the apartment we rented on Mount Washington,
on the top floor of the only three-story building in the
neighborhood. The couple who lived below us were also

renters. Around us were single-family brick homes, all modest but privately owned. The ground floor of our building housed a little grocery store, the only one you could find within a few blocks. Mama used to send me there for little items she needed for cooking.

Our apartment wasn't big. In the living area, the most conspicuous furniture was Tata's leather armchair, and it stood opposite a couch, which sagged in the middle. A coffee table between them held his newspapers and Mama's old fashion magazines. We had two bedrooms—mine was the small one—and one bathroom shared by everyone, including visitors.

Except for three pictures in the living area and the bedrooms, the apartment walls were bare. The pictures were all the same—a black Virgin Mary and baby Jesus with wide golden halos around their heads. Mama told me they weren't decoration, but they were beautiful, more so than a statue of a black Virgin Mary in their bedroom that she called "Black Madonna." More than once, she said the statue was a shrine, and she flanked it with candles in three cups that she always kept burning.

Spacious front and back porches saved the apartment from feeling cramped and suffocating. The back porch overlooked a small yard enclosed with a wooden fence. I never went into the backyard and I never saw anybody else who did. Half the porch served as storage for things we didn't often use.

Sometimes, we had guests who stayed a night or a few. Usually, they were relatives or visitors who also immigrated from Poland. They slept in the empty half where we kept two foldable cots and a chest of bed linens.

The front porch was mine. My play yard. My little kingdom. It had big windows all around, and when the ample, flowing, red linen curtains my mother made were drawn aside, it was the sunniest room. The few toys I had were all there. And when I became serious with my piano lessons, the used piano my parents bought me was placed there, too. We had to close the curtains when I wasn't practicing to keep the sunlight from cracking or bleaching it.

No other children lived in the apartment building or the houses near us, and I had no friends or playmates until I started school. I played with other children my age only when we visited relatives or friends.

We lived a quiet life ruled by daily routines from breakfast to bedtime. During my early growing-up years, I found those routines comforting.

But everything changed shortly after my eighth birthday.

My great aunt came. She was my mother's aunt, her father's sister. But every person younger than she called her Aunt Jola. At the time, I thought that was everyone in the whole world.

I disliked Aunt Jola at first because she kicked me out of my bedroom when she stayed with us—in my mind, a very long two months. To be fair, it was my parents who asked me to give up my room since Aunt Jola could not possibly sleep on a cot in the back porch. So I had to.

I balked and kept such a long face for several days that my mother had to set up a makeshift "room" for me. By the time Aunt Jola came, Mama had cleared an area on the front porch and shielded it with mismatched bed sheets hung like curtains. In the middle, she set up a cot cozy with my pillows and bed linens. My makeshift bedroom wasn't too bad. I even fantasized I lived in a fancy tent dressed in yards of fabric, where sultans or people like that lived in desert movies. But that was the daytime.

Nights were different. The apartment had uninsulated thin walls both inside and out and, at night, sleeping in the unheated porches was like camping out. Even in early spring, the cold seeped through blankets. So, my mother closed the inside doors to keep the heat within the living areas.

On my first night out on the porch, I snuck into my bedroom for my down comforter while the adults sat around the dinner table sipping vodka and soda water. They hardly noticed me. The comforter kept me warm but I could never get comfortable on the cot. I also felt very isolated from everyone inside the apartment and wondered many times if my mother would hear me and come to me if I had a nightmare.

*****

Aunt Jola had arrived like a storm. A storm in a bright purple suit with pink nails and stiff blonde hair, a few strands slipping from her French twist.

Three large suitcases came with her, hauled up sixteen steep steps by Tata. He had to sit and catch his breath after the second. Aunt Jola, herself, carried a handbag and a small box-like case that she hung on to until she was shown to my room to take it over.

She hugged and kissed everyone more than once. She came to me a third time but I stepped back.

"What a pretty little thing you are. You have the color of my hair."

"And my eyes," she added, touching my hair and staring long at me.

I shook her hands off my head and walked away to sit on a chair. With the dining table safely between us, I watched her, sizing her up and wondering why she was so special. She was colorful and bubbly, and in our quiet home, noisy and intrusive. My first impression justified my dislike of her.

Not long after she arrived, I learned why my parents believed she was so much better than every other friend or relative that she couldn't sleep out on the back porch. Before she fled to the United States, some years before World War II, she'd been a young concert pianist in Poland, sought out for her talent, youth, and beauty.

Here, she had no inkling what to do to get back into the concert circuit. She didn't speak English and knew little about the culture. She was just another ordinary young woman, fresh off the many boats from Europe that carried thousands like her.

At some point, she started giving piano lessons. Polish immigrants knew her, and a rich family of Polish Jews hired her to teach piano to their children. The rich family recommended her to others, including many who weren't Polish. They came to study with her and, eventually, she had enough pupils to make quite a good living teaching piano.

My parents were in awe of her talent, but they pitied her, too, because she was reduced to earning her keep with piano lessons. The glory of Aunt Jola's early years died on coming to a strange country where she could be safe and have a less uncertain future. I didn't grasp the tragic irony in her fate until a decade later.

In her mid-thirties, Aunt Jola married a widower with two children and a very good income. Less than a year later, they moved to Ohio, where her husband inherited some family property and business. When he died, she decided to come back to Pennsylvania to be closer to relatives. Her husband had left her well provided for.

She stayed with us until she could get her own place, a small house a few short blocks from where we lived. When she moved into it, all she had were a bed and two barstools to place by her kitchen counter. Contrary to Mama's expectation, the first big furniture that arrived was a gleaming new piano. The other pieces for the living and dining areas were delivered two weeks later.

Aunt Jola wanted to resume giving piano lessons, but not because she needed the money. I heard her and my mother talking in hushed voices the day before she moved to her house.

"I like having children around, maybe because I don't have my own."

"Why not? You were young enough and your husband was quite vigorous."

"John had children and he believed they were enough. I thought so, too, at first. But I couldn't think of them as mine. They resented me because I wasn't 'American.' When he and I married, I still had this thick accent. I was an outsider."

"Well, you should have had your own."

Aunt Jola seemed hesitant to answer.

"John was not ... you know .... We didn't do it very much. I actually thought he preferred ...."

She lowered her voice into a whisper although no one else was around and they didn't pay attention to me, playing in the porch. I didn't hear her, but I saw her shrug her shoulders.

"So, I never got pregnant."

Whatever Aunt Jola told her affected my mother visibly.

"I'd never have guessed that of John. Such an attractive man and well-built. And, he'd already been married once."

"Well, you never know, do you? I thought him very virile, which was what attracted me in the first place."

"I'm sorry it didn't turn out like you wanted it. At least, he lived with you, not ...."

"Oh, don't get me wrong. He was a truly nice person and very good to me. I had no doubt he loved me, in his own way. He loved listening to me play, which I did nearly every night for him. Me, I was crazy about him so I had to be content with what he could give me. Sadly, they didn't include children."

"Would you have married him if you knew?"

"I wondered about that later. I wanted children, so maybe not. Would you, if you were me?"

"Yes, because he's a good person and a good provider. That's enough for me. I think lasting marriages are based on friendship."

"What about Agnieszka?"

"I had her three years after Krzysztof and I were married. She was an accident. But, she's God's gift and we treasure her for that."

Aunt Jola's gaze sought mine. She winked at me and grinned at my mother.

"Maybe, you can lend me Agnieszka once in a while. She's such a pretty child with those blonde curls and sparkling blue eyes many of our first-born girls seem to always be blessed with."

She leaned a little backwards, her chin up in the air. She tossed her hair until the strands on her shoulders fell on her back.

"That didn't work in my case. And you, you're the youngest but you're blonde," my mother said, both hands on her head. She smoothed her own hair, dark brown and shiny, and gathered tidily in a bun at the nape of her neck.

"I guess I'm wrong, then. Kryztyna, your younger sister is blonde, too."

"Yes. I'm afraid Agnieszka is too much like her."

"Maybe she can come, play at my house. I have a backyard."

"We have a backyard here, as big as yours. But she doesn't go down there."

I learned to like Aunt Jola, in those peevish childhood years. I did hate her before I even met her. But she tried so hard to be nice, offering me treats and inviting me to sit on her lap. She didn't mind that I was already eight. Even Tata no longer let me do that. She wanted so much to be my friend.

Yes, I liked Aunt Jola, even loved her. She changed my life and left me a big part of herself, but she also caused me more misery than my mother did.

IV. Aunt Jola

After Aunt Jola was comfortably settled in her house, she invited relatives and their friends over for a late-afternoon party. She was giving a short recital to show her gratitude to those who welcomed her and helped her.

I saw Aunt Jola's house for the first time on the day of the party. Mama had gone there more than once to help her hang curtains and prepare some dishes for the party. Tata went once with a friend to move furniture.

A few people were already there when we arrived, and Aunt Jola was serving them drinks. She had left the door open, and we walked in after Tata pressed the doorbell. She came toward us when she saw us.

I was awestruck by the sight of her. She was dressed in a dark blue gown, shining with sequins around the bodice, and a silky skirt that flowed down to the floor. She wore matching high-heeled shoes. I had to raise my head higher so I could see her better. Her hair was up in a chignon, her face glowed, and she moved in the most regal way I ever saw. She seemed surrounded by a golden aura that set her apart from everyone else at that party, and if she had worn white, she would have been my idea of an angel or a fairy godmother.

In her most animated voice, Mama greeted Aunt Jola, breaking the spell she had cast on me.

"Aunt Jola! You're so lovely, and you can still fit in that gown."

"Well, actually I had it let out around the waist. Luckily there was all this fabric where the zipper is."

Aunt Jola laughed demurely and pointed to her side.

"I was barely eighteen when I wore this to a concert I gave and I have since put on ten pounds."

"Only ten! You're lucky."

"Well, maybe, that's one good thing about not getting pregnant and having a child."

She gazed at me and caressed my cheek, up and down, with the back of her hand. I turned my cheek away slowly. I didn't jerk my head like I used to.

"I would gladly give up my figure to have my own Agnieszka. You're a beautiful child, Agnes, did you know that?"

I smiled in delight that she called me by the English form of my name. My parents didn't seem pleased. I could tell they weren't about to call me 'Agnes.'

Aunt Jola led us into a large room where the grand piano stood smack in the middle. Around it, rented chairs had already been arranged. Pushed to the edge of the room were a couch and one ample armchair.

Mama said Aunt Jola had chosen this house for its large living room, which occupied more than half the whole house. The former owner had enlarged it by

knocking walls from a bedroom. The house was twice
the size of our apartment and had two bedrooms.

What I really envied was a second toilet and a
washstand attached to my aunt's bedroom. I wished I
had that little room. It would have made my life easier.
No waiting to go to the toilet.

An hour later, Aunt Jola announced she was ready
to start her recital. All her guests had arrived.

She approached my parents and me where we sat
in the third row. She took my hand and pulled me up.

"You'll be my inspiration tonight."

She stole a glance at my parents before she led me
to a chair in the first row. As I sat down, I looked back
at them and they smiled at me. But my mother was
scowling, her eyes dark and cold. She was displeased
with me, I thought. That was not new, but for the first
time, a chill went down my spine.

That recital was a turning point in my life. Until
then, I had heard music only from a tinny radio at
home, straining to blare out noisy songs. But music
from my aunt's grand piano transported me to my
childish idea of heaven. I've reminisced a lot over it
across the years and my memories would always be as
vivid as if that recital was unfolding before me.

Aunt Jola glided toward the piano, her chin held
high, her eyes directed straight ahead. She seemed to
forget she had an audience. Like a bird alighting on a
tree branch, she eased her figure onto the bench and
adjusted her gown. She paused, lifted the cover to the
piano, and paused again as she stared at the keys.
Watching her was like seeing a film in slow motion.

I held my breath until she raised her arms, her hands poised over the keyboard. She swept her fingers across the keys. Each note ran into the next, and together, they produced music that soared around the room, jolting me into paying attention. Her body swayed. Her arms and hands seemed to dance over the keys. Everything she did seemed part of the music.

I sat up straighter. My aunt had me under a spell once again. I was proud she singled me out, asked me to sit closest to her. I thought the recital was something I needed to go through—as I did many other doings my mother dreamed up. But from those beginning notes, I was caught.

I didn't grasp fully what I was going through. Not yet. Across the years, I understood more. But I was aware, even then, that my aunt's music sounded nothing like the faraway tinkle I heard on the radio. It was full, immediate, and arresting, drowning everything else around me. My body tingled, listening to it.

As abruptly as the first notes began, the music slowed and quieted to a hush, prodding me into a cocoon of my own thoughts. It kept on changing, as if my aunt was exploring the many ways to play those black and white keys. How could music be sad and happy at the same time? Or, soothe like a lullaby and tug at my insides until I was squirming in my chair? I closed my eyes and let the music take me somewhere I had never been.

Before those first soft notes could lull me completely, the piano keys seemed to collide again, for a few seconds. The tender caress of quiet notes alternated several times with the energy in swift sweeps of notes, as if they were talking to each other.

The music began its drawn-out end slowly, mounting into a frantic rush. My muscles clenched, my heart beat faster and faster, and heat coursed through my body. When I thought I could get more and more excited, the notes slowed until the music stopped.

When my aunt lifted her fingers off the piano keys, it seemed everyone, but me, let out one gigantic breath. Me? I was panting.

Everyone was quiet. Maybe, they expected Aunt Jola to take a bow. She did not. After a short pause, she began again with a few shorter pieces. They were quiet and slow, the kind you'd play alone at night. Now, of course, I would call them meditative. At that time, they made me both happy and sad.

Aunt Jola ended with another long piece more dramatic than the first. Her recital took an hour but, to me, it seemed short. By the time she finished, I was hungry.

The audience clapped loud and long but kept to their seats. Nobody dared to approach her. She stood next to her piano, proud, smiling, and swathed in her golden aura. But strangely distant. She bowed her head, her body still straight and upright.

She eased the cover down on the piano keys and walked toward me, her smile still frozen on her lips.

"Well, Agnieszka, how'd you like that?"

She was breathing hard. Her voice was soft and, standing closer to me, her eyes seemed moist and her mouth quivered a little. For the first time, I noticed her wrinkles and the sagging muscles on her cheeks. Up until she bowed her head, she was a fairy goddess to me but, at that moment, she seemed more human. More like Mama.

She caressed my cheek with the back of her hand and I knew, then, that I loved her.

"Well?"

"It's great. But I'm hungry."

What else could I have said? I was eight, still overwhelmed by music I had never heard and performance I had never seen.

"Were you thinking about food all the time I was playing? Your Mama should have given you something to eat."

"No. I mean your playing made me hungry."

She frowned, then she laughed and caressed my cheek again.

"Well, maybe, that's a good thing."

"I wanna learn to play, too. Like you."

"Now, that's a true compliment coming from the innocent mouth of a babe. Are you sure?"

"I wanna make people sad or excited, like you did."

"That takes a lot of work, you know, and you must want to do it."

She stared at me. Was she trying to read my mind?

"I'll work hard, I promise. It's my dream now. To play like you. I really, really wanna."

"You found that out after an hour, listening to me?"

I bobbed my head a few times.

"Well, if you really mean it, I guess we can work something out. Let me talk to your Mama."

*****

About a week later, my mother told me I was to go to my Aunt Jola's house after school.

"Aunt Jola will try to teach you to play. She thinks musical talent runs in our family. So, she's willing to spend some time to find out if you have the gift."

"She is? Oh, I'm so happy! Is it true? When can I start?"

"Tomorrow."

"I can't believe it. Isn't she the nicest, Mama?"

"Well, she does owe us. We put her up for two months. Anyway, we're family. We must help one another."

I was ecstatic. I wanted to jump up and down, but I'd been told that would disturb the tenants below us. So, I smiled. And kept smiling until my mother frowned at me.

"Don't expect too much. You might not have the gift."

Her remark dampened my smile.

"Aunt Jola's doing this out of the goodness of her heart, so work as hard as you can. If you don't have it, then you don't. You can always go to secretarial school."

I was taken aback.

"I'm not going to secretarial school. I wanna play the piano."

"If you don't have the gift, do you want to be a seamstress like me? I make good money but I don't get enough orders on a regular basis. Office work assures you a steady living."

"I wanna play the piano."

Not long after I started piano lessons, Aunt Jola told my mother I had the gift and should continue a while longer.

To me, she said, "You have promise. You're quick to pick up on what I've taught you"

"If I work really hard, can I play in concerts?"

"You have some fire in you—a great desire and even a kind of anger we can use. But to give concerts, you must practice for hours. You must keep on learning. Some kids are born with a musical gift."

"Do I have it, Aunt Jola?"

"Maybe; maybe not. It comes out pretty early, around five years old. But to be discovered, you need the chance to display it, which you didn't have. You had no musical instrument and your parents can't recognize talent staring them in the face."

"But can I learn to play as good as you, even if I don't have the gift?"

"I'm sure you can. You may have to work harder, but you're ahead already. You've got me as a teacher. I'll teach you all I know."

"I'll spend hours and hours practicing. I'll work really, really hard. You'll be proud of me. And one day, I'll give a concert, like you did."

"Oh, Agnieszka, my child."

"You're my angel, Aunt Jola."

I beamed at her and gave her a huge hug. She hugged me back and kissed me on both cheeks.

V. Growing

For four years, I worked hard to please Aunt Jola. She insisted I needed to practice for long hours and, without a piano at home, I had to do it at her house.

I didn't see my mother much after school and often, I came home excited but tired. We grew farther apart. My father was never home at daytime, so practice hours made no difference to him.

Tata was a puzzle to me those early years. All I could remember was he sat on his armchair in late afternoon and evening, his face hidden behind newspapers. I only had enough time to greet him at breakfast. He didn't talk much during our half-hour dinner, but he did smile at me whenever he caught me watching him, and he never failed to answer my questions. My problem was I could think of little to ask him.

I sometimes longed for when I was much younger. When I was little, Tata let me sit on his lap while he read his paper after dinner, if I didn't fidget around and disturb him. I always fell asleep, nestled in comfort against his chest. I woke up in the morning, tucked snugly in bed.

My mother had always been at home, sending me off to school, and waiting with a small glass of milk and a small cookie when I returned—just enough, she

insisted—to sustain me until dinner, two hours away.
She often sat with me at the dining table, as I ate and
drank. Sometimes, she talked about her day or asked
me about school, but she never asked me how my piano
lessons went, and never once said she wanted to hear
me play.

Still, when Aunt Jola announced I was ready to
give a recital, along with her two other pupils, my
mother seemed eager enough to go. She sewed me a
beautiful new dress and helped Aunt Jola with writing
and sending invitations.

I was very nervous about my first recital. Aunt Jola
had scheduled me to perform after her other two
pupils. I was older, had been taking lessons longer, and
I was anxious to play better than them.

Besides, I had to escape secretarial school. I
confess I didn't know much about it, but Mama made it
sound boring and tedious, something one must put up
with to survive. Was I to blame if, at twelve, a future
life, typing and filing, frightened me?

The recital was held in a small room my aunt
reserved at the community center. The audience
consisted of relatives and friends, all strangers to me
except for my parents. I didn't care what they thought
about my playing. Aunt Jola's opinion was all that
mattered.

I sat chewing my nails, stealing glances at the
other two performers. I had not met them, but I
sometimes had glimpses of the boy whose lessons
finished just as I was coming in for mine.

When my turn came, my hands and arms were shaking as I sat before the piano. I was painfully conscious of eyes directed at me. But I remembered Aunt Jola staring at the keyboard for a while before she started to play. So, I did the same and, after a minute or two, those black and white keys held my attention and in my head, I could hear the piece I was about to play flowing out from them. I thought it a miracle then. Later, I realized I could concentrate by staring at the keys.

My fingers began to caress those keys. The audience had become a blur. I was alone in the room with the music soaring out of a large instrument over which I had complete control.

As I stood and bowed before the audience at the close of my five-minute piece, I could sincerely say I played rather well and performed best among Aunt Jola's pupils.

My parents hugged me, without a word, but I read pride in their eyes. My Aunt Jola hugged me, too, and her eyes were moist.

Aunt Jola wiped her eyes with her flimsy hand kerchief. She said, "Well done for a first performance. If you continue to get better, you could play at a concert hall a few years from now."

A stranger came up from behind and patted me on the shoulders.

"Really nice, kid. You play with feeling."

Before I could thank him, he walked away. I stared at his lean form. He joined the family of the pupil I often saw leaving while I was coming in. I never saw his face. He left within a few minutes after embracing and talking to the boy.

At night, my mother came to my room. I sat on the bed, leaning on the headboard, studying my music sheets. I couldn't sleep, still too excited from my afternoon performance. She stood by my bed.

"Put those away now. It's bedtime."

I shoved the sheets into the drawer of my night table.

"My aunt thinks you have a future in music. But, you know, she herself never got to play at a concert here."

I knitted my brow for that puzzled look I had perfected by then, to get her to say more, without me uttering a word.

"I'm proud of you. Really, I am and I want the best for you. But we should also be realistic. We can never tell about the future."

"You don't think I can be a concert pianist? Aunt Jola thinks I can."

"I'm not saying that. Your aunt is extremely talented and she makes my hair stand on end whenever she plays. She was so talented she was doing concerts at sixteen in Poland and making good money, but here she got nowhere except to give lessons."

"She was young. She didn't know what to do and didn't speak English when she first got here."

"Yes, I know. Our country was in turmoil and, for years, grandfather feared war was coming. He wanted us all to leave, but he only had enough money for Aunt Jola and my family. I was a child, but I understood."

I had already heard my mother's story, and I was too distracted to listen to it again. All I could think about was playing piano.

"Aunt Jola thinks I should try out for one of the conservatories in two years."

"We don't have the money."

"But if I'm accepted, she says I get to experience what it's like to play with other talented musicians. Then, I get better and can audition for an orchestra or a chamber group. I can make money."

"Maybe, but before that, you'll need money for school."

"She says I can try for a scholarship."

"I see. Well, we'll keep talking about it. You still have time."

She bent toward me and gave me a peck on the forehead, her lips cold and dry. She turned to leave, but at the door, she stopped.

"You did play beautifully. Maybe your aunt is right. But don't set your heart on it. You could end up disappointed."

"I refuse to be a typist."

I pushed my lower lip into a petulant pout.

"Well, you can give lessons. She's done well enough supporting herself on those."

Mama left me feeling let down. I was ecstatic at Aunt Jola's confidence in me. She had allowed me to dream that someday I could play in a concert. Mama's remarks brought me close to tears. Did she care how I felt, what mattered to me? Didn't she want me to succeed?

Months later, as I undid the ties on my apron after washing the dinner dishes, Mama took hers off, too. Usually, I left her puttering in the kitchen and I went to my room to study, but it was the night before I started my last year at junior high and I had no homework. I was going to study my music sheets and read. She followed me to my room.

"We need to talk."

We sat down on the edge of my bed. She took my hand in both of hers and held it. What she was going to say was important to her.

"I'll say this to you just once. You're growing fast. Why, in the past, you'd be considered a woman, ready to have children. You will be on your own in a few very short years and I won't be there to guide you. I've given you a home, fed you, clothed you, and sent you to school. I've been raising you to be an upstanding American I could be proud of, and done my best to teach you decency and respect toward others, especially your elders. You owe much to those who've made you who you are and you must give something back in return."

She stopped, gave me a peck on the cheek, and let my hand go. She regarded me for some moments, sizing me up.

"Let your conscience be your guide, Agnieszka. If you learned all I've taught you, you'll do well."

She stood up, smiled, and walked toward the door. There, she stopped.

"Good night and sweet dreams."

"Good night," I murmured, in confusion.

What was I supposed to say?

"Oh, one more thing. Tata and I decided to get you a used piano so you can practice here, as long as you like. We shouldn't bother your grandaunt more than we have to."

She didn't wait for me to answer and was gone before I reached the door to close it.

I sat on my bed, puzzling over her words. What could she really mean? How much more was I supposed to do to live up to her idea of an "upstanding American?" My grades were reasonably good, I had always followed rules, and I wasn't one of the "wild" or "loose" girls in school.

If she held me to the same rigid code she lived by, I was sure to disappoint her. I began to worry.

I heard from Mama once that she tried to become "American" when she first arrived here. She failed, painfully. To protect herself from future hurts, she never allowed herself to get close to anybody. She built a wall, setting her apart from others

Why couldn't I grow a wall? Protect myself from her impossible expectations? If it worked for her, it should for me, too. From then on, except at breakfast and dinner, I isolated myself in my room and watched what I said and did in Mama's presence. But I soon found that my efforts were wasted. To begin with, she rarely asked about what I did or how I felt. She didn't seem curious about school, my piano playing, or my few acquaintances. Looking back on it a few years later, I realized she had already created a wall between us, farther back than I could remember.

The used piano was delivered a few days later. A small, scratched up instrument so unlike Aunt Jola's gleaming grand. But it was mine. I'd close the door to the front porch and escape into my music whenever I could.

The following day, after my lesson, Aunt Jola sent me home.

"I have a new pupil. She'll be here in fifteen minutes. Go home and practice for two hours."

"Can't I stay and practice until she comes?"

"I'm sorry, no. I promised your mother I'll send you home as soon as you're done."

"But our piano doesn't sound as good as yours."

"Well, no it wouldn't. But your technique and the notes should still be the same. Anyway, it's merely for practice. When you come back tomorrow, we'll start with the piece you practiced and I can tell you what I think. Now, go."

I walked home in a sour mood. I was sure my mother wanted more control over me and my aunt was going along with it.

*****

Aunt Jola's pupils gave a recital at the same place every year. By my eighth year studying piano with her, our group had grown to six. After the recital that year, I reminded Aunt Jola about my applying to a conservatory.

"It's time, isn't it, Aunt Jola? I'm now sixteen. Don't you think I should be ready?"

"If we're talking about your progress, I think you were ready last year. But your mother insisted that you finish high school. And she's right. Now, when you go, you'd be in college. In this city, there are two places you could apply to, to continue your training."

"I finish high school next year. You started doing concerts at sixteen. The way I'm going, I'll be in my twenties before I can do that."

"Impatient. Impatient. You started late and it's much more competitive here. I lived my early youth in a different time and a different country. My parents loved music and we had a piano at home when I was a kid. My mother gave me my first lessons when I was four. I was considered something of a child prodigy."

"You're lucky."

"I know I was."

"You've never talked about your parents. What happened to them? Were they nice?"

"They died in the war. They were the best."

"Why did they stay behind?"

"Not enough money. My parents did all they could so all their children could come here. Your grandparents and me were fortunate enough. Everyone decided my talent entitled me to go and I was the youngest child. I was eighteen. Your grandparents went because they had two children and your grandmother was pregnant with her third. There was no question the children must go."

"How old was my mother when she came?"

"Eight, I think. Hasn't she ever told you the story?"

"Years ago. We don't talk much. I knew she was very young. Actually, I don't remember much of what she told me. It was dark and she slept a lot, her brother's arms around her."

"I'm not surprised. She was probably too young to remember. We were uncomfortable on the ship, had some big waves that made most of us puke, and swear never to be on another ship again. Apart from that, the trip was quite boring. It was the years that followed which were very hard."

Aunt Jola scowled and compressed her lips. Her mind had drifted away, back to the suffering and humiliation of that earlier time. I had learned to read her gestures well, by then. The muscles on her face were quivering in anger and self-pity.

I wanted to hear more but people—friends and families of her pupils—were milling about. I'd have to ask her some other time.

Aunt Jola regained her composure, minutes later.

"Let me talk to your mother about music school. I have some brochures I collected from two or three places."

"I can talk to her about it. You can lend me your brochures. The school counselor told me she'd help me fill out and send forms."

"It's a bit more complicated than that. You'll need to audition, and different schools have varying requirements for admission."

A few days later, to my distress, I found that not only was it complicated, it sounded impossible.

I came home from the supermarket on an errand for Mama, hauling two bags of groceries up two flights of stairs. My legs and arms were groaning and I was sweating from the walk. Near the top, I put the bags down on the floor in front of me before I climbed the last five or six steps. As I bent to pick up the bags, I heard Mama's and Aunt Jola's loud voices in the kitchen.

"You've filled her head with impossible dreams."

"And you've never allowed her to dream."

"How dare you say that? She's my daughter. I want what's best for her."

"I'm sorry. Of course, you do. That was uncalled for. I've asked you since last year if she could start applying to music school. But you keep putting off talking about it."

"We don't have the money for tuition."

"Is that the only problem? There are scholarships and financial aid."

"What if she doesn't get in?"

"I think she will, at one of those schools. I was confident she's been ready since last year. We could try the local ones first. If she doesn't get into those, she can try others not far from here or try again next year. If she started last year, she would already have some experience applying and I would have some idea how to help her get admitted. We could have been working on her weak areas."

"Without a scholarship, she can't go. We don't have the money to send her."

"If she gets into the academy here, she can live at home."

"What if she doesn't? Even if she gets a scholarship somewhere else, we need money to pay for her living expenses. We can't afford it."

"I'll lend you some money to pay for her expenses."

"We can't pay you back. We're not rich like you. We have very little money in the bank."

"Give her a chance. She has talent. She'll make you proud."

"I don't need you to tell me that. Like I said, she's my daughter. I know her and what's best for her."

"No question."

"You know what my problem is? You've filled her head with dreams. Pipe dreams. Now, I have to teach her to come down to earth. But you have a problem, too. You know what it is? You don't have a child of your own. So, you want mine."

Minutes followed when neither spoke. Then, I heard Aunt Jola's quivering voice.

"What a cruel thing to say. It's true I love Agnes, from the moment I saw her and, maybe, I wished she was the daughter I could have had. But I'm well aware she's yours and not mine."

"Then, don't tell me what to do."

Aunt Jola didn't answer. I heard a chair scraping against the floor and footsteps rushing from the kitchen. I pressed my body against the wall next to the stairwell. Within seconds, Aunt Jola came striding through the door, pain and anger written on her face.

She ran down the stairs and banged the entrance door shut.

I waited a few seconds and descended the stairs as noiselessly as I could. Halfway down, I sat on the steps. I wanted to cry. Shout. Hit the wall. Anything to vent my frustration. I felt dejected and hopeless about my future. I was not going to the conservatory. In fact, I wasn't going anywhere.

I fought an urge to run outside, but I had nowhere to go. I didn't want to talk to anyone, not even Aunt Jola. Then, I remembered the groceries. Mama needed them to prepare dinner, which Tata expected at a specific hour.

I gritted my teeth, walked back up the stairs and picked up the bags of groceries. To announce my presence so Mama would think I just came in, I banged the door between the porch and the kitchen to close it behind me. In the kitchen, I deposited the bags on the counter without saying a word.

"There you are. I was wondering when you'd ever get here. You took so long. I won't have enough time to prepare dinner before Tata gets home."

Her voice sounded like it always did—low, quietly reproachful, and no hint of the angry exchange between her and my aunt. I turned my back to her, and without a word, went straight to my room. I lay on the bed, mulling over what I heard. I grew angrier by the minute.

I bounced from my bed and marched back into the kitchen, my hands clenched into fists. My eyes and my cheeks blazed with anger I could hardly control.

"I don't belong to you. I don't belong to Aunt Jola. I belong to me. You can't tell me what to do."

I thought my voice was low and collected, but I was probably shouting. My behavior was unusual, even to me. To my mother, it was unconscionable.

I saw a palm swinging across my cheek. I reeled back against the kitchen counter, my left cheek aflame with pain. I didn't cry but regarded my mother with narrowed eyes. She had never laid a hand on me. At that moment, I really hated her. I spun around and walked slowly back to my room. I didn't come out for dinner and neither my mother nor my father summoned me to the table.

Mama and I avoided each other the next few days and I didn't go to Aunt Jola's house for piano lessons. I felt adrift. The one dream I had set my heart on was dead. One year away from graduating and I could look forward to nothing but typing and filing.

I made mostly Bs and a couple of Cs in school. I could have gotten better grades but I neglected school to practice piano for hours. For that, I blamed Aunt Jola. I believed her and focused my efforts and hopes on one dream. With better grades, I might have gone to a good college and studied to become a teacher.

But could I have? Forces or circumstances outside my control could always crush my dreams to dust. As they had done to my future in music.

I remembered my mother's words the night after my first recital. She cautioned me not to dream too high, to be realistic in what I could aspire to, and to be prepared for the same mundane existence she had.

Those words now seemed wise and I should thank her. She was right, after all. They had no money for the professional training I needed, so I had little chance at a career in music or anything above what high school prepared me for. But I could not be grateful for the death of a dream, or for a bleak future. Not at sixteen; not in my eagerness and youth.

I resented my mother. I believed her to be indifferent to my dream. Worse, she attempted to kill it. She had never supported me, never cheered my attempts to master the piano. She claimed she didn't want me disappointed. But as I saw it then, the truth was she did not want me to succeed. She preferred to keep me where she was.

That evening, I began to sense that I was a pawn, tossed around in a continuing rivalry between Mama and Aunt Jola—two women plagued by personal frustrations and unfulfilled dreams.

VI. Music and Me

I kept away from Aunt Jola's house for two weeks. I returned the following Wednesday after school. A young man with thick dark curly hair and tan complexion opened the door. I stood four inches above five feet and he wasn't much taller.

"Are you here for lessons?" He sounded irritated.

"Yes. Who are you? Are you a new student?"

"No, I'm not. I'm here to pick up my brother after his lessons. He and Mrs. Armey are in the middle of one. She asked me to see who's at the door. She didn't seem to be expecting anyone. But, I guess you'd better come in."

"I'm early and I was gone for two weeks."

I decided to ignore him and walked past him to the kitchen. There, I could wait without disturbing his brother's session. I sat on a barstool and placed my bag on the floor.

He followed me there.

"I'm early, too. One of my classes was cancelled so I decided to hear my brother play, but you interrupted. He has twenty minutes more. You'll have to wait."

"No problem. I can do my homework."

I pulled a notebook and a ballpoint pen from my bag and started my homework. If he saw me busy, he would return to the living room to listen to his brother.

Or, so I guessed, but he didn't budge. Instead, he stared at me for some moments.

His eyes lit up and he broke into a smile.

"I remember you. You were at that first recital. You played last. The serious one who poured her heart out into a piece I thought a bit too mature for someone no more than eleven years old."

He unabashedly looked me up and down. I felt very self-conscious. His smile broadened.

"You've grown."

"A lot can happen in four years. And I was twelve, not eleven."

He had an infectious smile, and I couldn't help returning it. I smiled reluctantly, shyly, too confused to think of anything more to say. Nobody had ever regarded me the way he did, and I found it unnerving. But it was also exciting, a new and strange sensation that left me breathless, tingly all over, and conscious, for the first time, of his smiling dark brown eyes under thick dark lashes. They were beautiful.

He was charming. And he aroused my curiosity, although I had meant to ignore him.

"Well, so you decided to come back," I heard my aunt say.

I was relieved to see her. She rescued me from having to talk to this young man. And yet, I was a tad irritated that she came at the very moment I discovered that he was fascinating.

Aunt Jola gave me a quick peck on the cheek and turned to him.

"That piece she played at her first recital was a Liszt *Liebestraum*. I told her it didn't seem appropriate for one so young but she insisted. She did pretty well, though, for one lacking experience in both life and the piano."

"I do know the piece. Dreams of love. Like my brother, I had lessons when I was a child but I never took to music the way he has. I love classical music, though, especially Liszt."

"Well, Mr. Weisz, tell us your first name. I know about you from Robbie. He assures me you pick him up after his lessons but I've never seen you before."

"I have to rush from my classes at the university and I often get here a few minutes after his lesson. My name is Leonard but Leonard sounds like some pompous old man. So, please call me Lenny."

He shook my aunt's hand.

"Lenny, you may call me Aunt Jola. Everybody does, including my pupils. This young woman here is Agnes Talar or Agnieszka as her parents prefer to call her. Her mother is my brother's daughter. That makes her my grandniece."

My aunt surprised me. She was the first to ever refer to me as a "young woman." To my parents and teachers, I was often just "she" or, sometimes, "child," "girl," "daughter," "niece," or "pupil." I was pleased Aunt Jola thought of me as a "young woman," but I was also uneasy, conscious that I wasn't that person yet. I needed a lot more maturing before I became her.

Lenny hesitated for an instant before extending his hand to me.

"Nice to meet you, Agnieszka. I like your name. It's beautiful and unusual."

I took his hand in confusion and embarrassment, surprised by his compliment. My heart beat a little faster.

"Well, maybe we should have some soda while Robbie practices his new lesson. You're not in a hurry to be home, are you Agnes?"

Lenny was staring at me, a little too intently for my comfort, and I took a moment to answer.

"No, Mama doesn't know I'm here."

"But you've come for your lessons."

"Yes, if that's okay. Let me help you with the glasses, Aunt Jola."

Lenny continued staring at me, and I was feeling more uncomfortable by the minute. If I moved around, I thought he'd look elsewhere. I took three glasses from a kitchen cabinet and ice cubes from the freezer. My aunt filled the glasses with soda water and motioned for us to sit on the barstools.

Aunt Jola and Lenny carried on a conversation I hardly listened to. I slowly sipped my soda, more anxious to talk to my aunt about what had been troubling me than to practice or go through lessons that afternoon. But I wasn't going to say anything while Lenny, a nosey stranger, was there.

Later, after Lenny and Robbie left, Aunt Jola led me back to the sofa.

"You'd know, by now, what came out of my talking to your mother about you going to a conservatory."

"Yes. I overheard you two. Since I was a child, you, two, have had this habit, talking as if I wasn't there."

"I didn't see you."

"You never did, but this time, I didn't want you to notice me."

"I didn't expect you to come back here after that. Your Mama was quite definite that my help isn't wanted."

"I don't know why I came. I have no future in music. So, why practice?"

My voice quivered. I was so close to tears. Aunt Jola didn't answer, but her sad eyes told me she sympathized with me.

"I guess I feel more at home here. Mama and I haven't said ten words to each other the past two weeks."

"You're probably angry with her right now. But she's your mother and she does love you."

I burst out crying then.

"I hate her. I think she wants me to be like her. A bitter woman who resents everything. But, I'm not gonna be like her. I'm just not."

"That's no way to talk about your Mama, Agnes."

"She slapped me, you know, after you two argued."

"I'm so sorry. She was angry and frustrated and she may have taken it out on you. I don't always know why she does what she does, but I know she's had a hard life. So, try to understand where she's coming from."

"I can be angry, too. But who do I have to take it out on? And why should I try to understand her? She doesn't bother to ask what I think or how I feel."

"I have no answers for you, Agnes. All I can say is bear with your Mama. Life was tough when we arrived, a real comedown from what she was used to in Poland. This country was still reeling from the depression. For two years, we were cramped in one room in a cousin's small apartment. We spoke no English and Ania's father couldn't find a job. I was luckier, as you know, because music is a universal language and I could teach it by showing pupils what to do."

I averted my eyes as I began to feel some remorse. I never went through the same hardships Mama did. For some reason, coming from Aunt Jola, the story of their early years in this country sounded more moving. Or, maybe, I was just older and was no longer as self-centered.

"When my brother finally found a job, he couldn't make enough to support his family comfortably. Ania had to go through many months of deprivation. I think my brother grew more bitter by the day. His wife, your grandmother, also had a difficult delivery and they were in debt for years with medical bills."

"Was that Aunt Kryztyna who was born? I've never met her."

"She lives with her husband in Washington, on the West Coast."

"Mama doesn't talk to her."

"I'm not surprised. Ania resented her sister."

"Is that why she doesn't write or call her? Aunt Kryztyna sends Christmas cards every year. That's it. She used to send me cards and money on my birthday. But she stopped a few years ago."

"She must have her reasons. I give her credit for even doing that much. The break with your Mama was pretty bad."

"Really? Mama doesn't talk about it. What happened?"

"Well, you see, Kryztyna was prettier and smarter. She went to college. In her second year, your grandfather passed away and Ania had to support her. She expected Kryztyna to help the family when she got her degree. But she fell in love with a classmate from Washington, married him, and they left for Seattle soon after. To make matters worse, he wasn't Catholic and Ania accused her sister of renouncing her faith."

"Huh? That's a problem? Are we supposed to marry only Catholics?"

"Many people believe you don't marry outside your faith. Your Mama's like that. She's very devout, but I think she feels uneasy about being Catholic. She had some bad experience in school—an English teacher who hated Catholics. Assigned Ania's class to read the *Pit and the Pendulum*, about a man, tortured by zealous Spanish inquisitors. She harped on about all the awful things Catholics had done throughout history and Ania often came home very upset. Her classmates avoided her after they read that story."

"She never told me that story. Poor Mama. I can see why she'd be upset. At school, no one cares. We've never talked about religion in class."

"People are more liberal now."

"She had an older brother. What happened to him? Mama doesn't talk about him."

"At twenty-two, right after he became a citizen, he enlisted and went to war. He was killed not too long after, in late 1943. Things might have been different had he lived."

"How sad. So young. What was he like?"

"He was smart, planned to go to college, raise the family out of poverty. It was part of his plan to join the military so he'd have money for college, maybe law school. He protected Ania, and she worshipped him. She was about your age when he died."

"Maybe, her dreams died with him."

"We've all had dreams that went nowhere."

"You, too, Aunt Jola?"

"Mine, too, as soon as we left Poland."

Aunt Jola sighed; her eyes shone with tears she held back. She forced a smile.

"But I had my piano training and only myself to take care of. Ania was too young, unskilled. The burden meant for her brother was too much for her. She wasn't prepared to take it on. And I'm sure she feels she got no thanks for her sacrifice."

Mama's past did help me understand her better, but I didn't feel any more forgiving of her or more accepting of my fate. I actually felt more hopeless than ever. The recent loss of my dreams still troubled me. I lived in a world constricted by want of money, not enough affection from my mother, and anxieties that I would be like her.

I practiced that afternoon, feeling adrift, and haunted by my lost dreams and uncertain future.

"You fumbled, here and there. But there was more heart in in your playing than I've ever heard from you."

My aunt smiled. Her eyes were moist.

I felt it, too—that heart she was talking about. I had not touched my used piano at home since the afternoon my mother slapped me. At Aunt Jola's house, I played with all I had in me. I didn't care if my fingers faltered a little or that my aunt was listening for flaws in my playing.

I poured all my frustrations, my unhappiness, my uncertainties into Beethoven's *Appasionata*. I chose what to play that afternoon and my aunt didn't object. The drama in that piece suited my own state of mind— a state that fought against what I saw as my fate. Were my dreams really shattered? In my music at least, I could be defiant, pour all my passion onto those keys.

Before my aunt could tell me what she thought, I followed the piece with Beethoven's *Pathetique*. For me, those pieces were somehow related.

For the first time, I was conscious I played for myself alone, that I did not have to do so in service of a dream. I played for me. For how the music I could make with the piano intensified and then soothed my pain. For how it blotted out everything and became my whole world while it lasted. For how it promised to be the nurturer and savior of my soul.

VII. First Love

"Agnes!"

I heard someone calling as I walked from school toward my aunt's house. I had slipped back into the habit of staying hours at her house to practice on her grand. Mama never asked me where I'd been when I came home, but she always left the cookie and milk on the table for me to consume alone.

"Agnes."

The voice was male and adolescent—breaking from a child's high pitch into the low timbre of a man's. It was approaching me from behind, accompanied by hurried footsteps.

"Agnes."

A moist warm hand touched my arm and I realized the "Agnes" being called was me. I was so unused to the name and only answered to it when I heard it coming from my aunt's lips, at her house. She'd been careful, for some time now, not to use it when my parents were around.

"Robbie! What are you doing here?"

"I'm with my brother. You remember Lenny? He's waiting in that blue car over there. We've come to take you to the hospital."

"The hospital? Why? What's the matter?"

"Your aunt's at the hospital. An ambulance took her there."

"Is she all right?"

"I think so, but she was pale and gasping for breath. I called emergency because she asked me. She had chest pains during my exercises. She told me where to find you and to get you, but I had to wait for my brother. He says we have to hurry. She's been at the hospital for about half an hour."

We ran toward Lenny's car, and in those few seconds, I kept thinking—I couldn't lose my aunt. She was all that was left of my dreams. I was shaking and breathing hard by the time I climbed into the backseat, the first time I felt truly afraid.

"Hello, Agnes. I'm sorry our second meeting is not under better circumstances." Lenny glanced at me as if he sensed my fear. "I'm sure they'll take good care of her at the hospital."

I stared mutely at him.

"You must be very close to your aunt."

"She believes in me."

If he was waiting for me to say more, I disappointed him. I was trying to make sense of this unexpected event. Besides, my mother taught me well: Never disclose strong feelings to a stranger. He could use them to hurt you.

It was inevitable that my aunt and I grew quite close from those nearly daily sessions we had. Particularly during the many difficult and frustrating hours, when we were probably most naked to each other. I made mistakes and disappointed her, but she stayed patient with me and understood how I felt.

We had many good moments, too. Moments of discovery wondrous to a child living in a small world. And when she beamed at me and I realized I had mastered a piece, I glowed for hours. I loved Aunt Jola, I told myself that afternoon. I was grateful that she had given me music and taught me to play. She was the very first person to show me what I could do and what I could reach for.

The hospital kept my aunt overnight for observation and more tests. They released her the next day with pills and a diagnosis of heart disease.

My mother and I brought her home from the hospital. Lenny drove us. The day before, he had offered to take me back to the hospital. He arrived promptly to pick me up at Aunt Jola's house and didn't seem surprised to see Mama waiting with me.

On our return home from the hospital, Aunt Jola sat in the back, pale, subdued, and spaced out. For someone who always had something to say, her behavior was sad and disturbing. Mama could sit in silence for hours, but not Aunt Jola. If she could not talk, she would hum to herself or, if she was home, she would put on some classical music. She would have no qualms asking Lenny to turn on his car radio. Sounds were important to Aunt Jola.

My mother decided to stay with her on her first night back from the hospital. She needed her housedress, slippers and a few toiletries and Lenny drove me the few blocks to our apartment to get them.

Later in the afternoon, we left my mother with Aunt Jola and he drove me home again, although I told him he didn't need to. In front of our building, he turned off his car.

"Don't worry too much about your aunt. She should be back to normal if she takes her pills and does what the doctor prescribes. Usually, a team—all health care professionals—helps patients like her. My grandmother survived another fifteen years after she was diagnosed."

"I can't help worrying about Aunt Jola. I don't know what I'd do without her. She taught me all I know about music, what it can do for me. She's closer to me than my mother."

"She'll be okay, you'll see. Your aunt's a survivor."

"Thank you for saying that. I'm really worried about her. She seemed so different this morning. And thank you for taking me home."

I pushed down the door handle on the car so I could get off. Before I could open the door, Lenny touched my knee. I froze.

"Don't go yet," he said.

He withdrew his hand. I couldn't move and I didn't dare look at him, much less say anything.

"This may not be the time to say this, but I might not get another chance."

I lifted my hand from the handle, placed it on my lap, and waited.

"I want to see you again. I asked your aunt for your telephone number but she wouldn't give it to me. She said your parents won't approve; that they're old-fashioned and probably wouldn't let you go out with me."

My cheeks were burning and my heart was thumping. When we first met, I sensed some strong connection between us that got me muddle-headed and breathless. Later, on that same day and alone in my room, I thought about our meeting and admitted to myself that I had a crush on him. The first time I was ever attracted to a man.

But I neither imagined nor hoped he'd be interested in me. He was, after all, already in college, and seemed too mature and sophisticated to care for a high school teenager like me. I was content admiring him from afar, certain that my feelings for him would fade with time and inattention.

I had never gone out with a guy before and I was too naïve to know how to respond. What did a woman say to a man interested in her? I racked my brain for some clever words but ended up just waiting for Lenny to speak again.

"I should tell you I'm twenty-one, five years older than you. That might seem like a lot to you and I did tell myself you're too young. But, in a couple of years, maybe less, that difference may no longer matter. Anyway, believe it or not, I can't help thinking about you. I can't tell if it's my image of an earnest twelve-year old, making love to a piano, four years ago. Or, if it's the beautiful young woman you've become, and I can't tear my eyes off the bluest eyes I've ever seen."

What was I supposed to say to all that? I, who had no clue and lived in a world within the small perimeter of my parent's home—Aunt Jola's, the school, and the neighborhood supermarket. And he, a man, not a boy, who found me attractive, couldn't help thinking about me, and wanted to see me again. Was I speechless because he stirred desire in me, too?

"I take it you've never been out with a boy. For an ice cream or a soda maybe, or a movie?"

I shook my head.

"Not even with your friends?"

I shook my head again.

"I had my first girlfriend at fourteen. She was my age and we were in the same class. It was all for fun and for bragging to other boys in the group we always went with to the ice cream parlor or the soda fountain."

I was curious. He described a world unfamiliar to me.

Whenever I was too impatient to listen to recordings of pieces before learning them, Aunt Jola always said, "The more you listen, the more you know. The more you know, the better you understand. Then, you play better." Why could it not apply to any situation? I found the courage to speak.

"How long did you go steady?"

"Oh, a few months. I had three more by the time I graduated from high school."

"I haven't had fun like that. After school, I go to my aunt's for piano. On weekends, after homework, I do more of the same thing. I never wondered if I was missing something."

"Yes, the piano requires your undivided dedication, if you want to excel in it. That's why I couldn't stick to it. I wanted to experience as much as I could of life."

"The piano was going to be my life."

"Was? Are you abandoning it?"

"No, not totally. I don't think I can. But it can't be my life. My aunt tells me I'm highly talented, but I have to work to be exceptional."

"Even someone with an exceptional gift has to practice and keep learning."

"Yes. I need to continue my studies, but my parents can't afford it."

"What about scholarships?"

"They tell me it's not enough to get me through music school."

"Please, let's not talk about it anymore." The wound from my lost dream was still too raw and his understanding brought unbidden tears to my eyes.

"Okay. But I'd like to be around in case you do. I guarantee you'll find me sympathetic."

He smiled, tenderly, sweetly, and held my gaze. I was mesmerized. This man who awakened strong, confusing, exciting sensations in me, was also the first to make me feel I truly mattered. The real Me, apart from my music. Apart from my role as daughter to old parents who probably expected me to stay around to care for them in their waning years.

"So, can I see you again? Talk over a soda or ice cream sundae, if you wish. Get to know each other better and later, if we become more comfortable with each other, we could go to a movie or go dancing."

"I'll go out with you," I blurted out in a moment of daring and defiance, a moment I had to seize before it could pass me by in the blink of an eye.

"Are you sure? What about your parents?"

I shrugged. "Maybe, they won't object. I won't know until I do it."

Inwardly, I decided they were not going to know about it.

*****

For some weeks after that, Lenny came on Friday afternoons to pick me up from school and take me to the same place for soda. Those first meetings came by quite easily and I didn't need excuses to give my mother. Aunt Jola was taking about a month or so recovering and learning how to live with her illness, and she suspended our lessons. Mama assumed I went to her house to help her after school.

Much of my life went on as before, but I was aware I was changing. Lenny was exposing me to so much that, to me, was new and fresh, though others my age probably took them for granted.

The soda fountain was noisy, full of families and young people out for fun together, the first afternoon I went there with Lenny. We had to jostle our way to the bar where servers prepared sodas or ice cream sundaes. He ordered ice cream sodas for us, and we claimed seats at the farthest end of the bar. Our first conversation was painful.

"How was school today?"

Lenny's voice was near shouting level.

"Okay, nothing new. Is it always like this here?"

"Everyday."

Lenny swirled the ice cream into the soda with his long spoon, but I didn't care much for the mixture so I scooped my ice cream first. He finished his soda before I did.

He said as he pushed his empty glass away, "What's your favorite subject?"

"I haven't got one. They're all the same."

"Who's your favorite teacher?"

"No one. They're all okay, I guess."

He asked all the usual questions about school, and then, he fell silent. The din made talking hard, but I had nothing much to say, in any case, unless it was about my music. We smiled at each other and watched the bustle going on around us.

Still, being at the soda fountain was exciting. It showed me how much I missed out while I devoted myself to the piano. To my classmates, being there was probably ordinary and dull.

We left after an hour. Our interaction had been dragging and awkward and I worried that Lenny might not want to see me again. I knew that I was eager to return to the soda fountain for the people, the noise, and the atmosphere. And because I wanted to get to know Lenny better.

I felt agitated in his presence, but at the fountain, I could hide my nervousness and ignorance. With the crowd all around us, I was anonymous and could pretend I wasn't so self-conscious. There, I felt safe being with him while I got used to the idea of having a beau.

A beau. Was Lenny my beau? I never thought I would have one, particularly someone already in college. I would definitely be the envy of my few not-so-close friends, once they learned about him.

The third time we were at the soda fountain, Lenny handed me a small brown shopping bag. In it was a 33-rpm LP record.

Lenny said, "It's Alicia de Larocha playing *Liebestraum* and *Hungarian Rhapsody #2*. It's one of my favorite records but now it's yours."

"You're giving it to me?"

"Something for you to remember me by."

"But won't you miss it?"

"I can borrow it whenever I miss it enough that I've got to listen to it again. *Liebestraum*, as you know, is dreamy, but *Hungarian Rhapsody* is dramatic and vibrant. Anyway, they're both played so beautifully that you forget what's going on around you."

"I can't take this. I can't play it at home. Even if I can, my mother will be nosey and ask me questions."

In fact, I wanted to keep it because he gave it to me and it had once been his. I could imagine him lying on his bed, lost in the beauty of the music.

"Your mother can't be that strict. Tell her you borrowed it from a friend."

"I could, but she wouldn't believe me. There's a bigger problem. We have no phonograph."

I blushed at that confession.

He stared at me, his mouth agape for a second or two.

"No phonograph? That's a problem. We'll have to think of something."

"Oh, I know. I won't take it home. I can leave it at my aunt's and play it there. She has a collection of classical piano music, including a couple by this pianist. She always makes me listen to a piece a few times before I learn it."

"Will she ask you where you got it?"

"I'll tell her the truth, and if I ask her not to tell Mama, she won't. Anyway, what's so wrong about me accepting a gift from you?"

"Nothing at all. But I don't want to get you into trouble."

I didn't mean for him to answer the question—it was for me, to convince myself to accept the gift without guilt. But, I smiled at him, grateful for his thoughtfulness.

I smiled. "The very first record I own. Thank you so much."

I held the record to my bosom. I also smiled in satisfaction that I found a way around my mother's rules. Strictly speaking, they were not rules. She never stated them as such but she could restrain me easily with her scowls, the way she pressed her lips tight, how rigidly she stood, and how her eyes almost dissolved into slits whenever she disapproved. That was how I learned Mama's "rules."

Lenny regarded me with his sweetest smile. For a few minutes, he kept silent and was thoughtful.

"Hmmm. It seems there's much I have to initiate you into. Wait here a minute."

He stood and walked to a big jukebox at the other end of the bar. After browsing through the offerings, he chose a song and popular music blared into the room.

"Do you know this song?" Lenny asked as he sat down.

I shook my head.

"It was quite popular, at the top of the chart, and the favorite in college campuses not so long ago. Everyone I know has the LP it's on. The singer has been making the round of colleges and I went to his concert at the university."

"Who's this singer?"

"Don McLean and the song is *American Pie*. My friends at school and I still argue about what it means. It's about three times as long as most songs and the lyrics are like poetry."

I listened closely to the music until it was finished. Lenny kept silent.

"I like it. It's a song about music and has phrasings that vary like classical music."

"It's actually also about what's happening in America and, maybe, about the loss of innocence in our generation."

"It's saying all that?"

I was intrigued. The piano pieces I'd learned had little to say about current conditions in my world.

"I think so. A friend of mine says she has a classmate who's doing a paper on it. I can get you the

song on a 45, if you like, although they break it up to
fit those small records."

"No, please, don't spend anymore to get me a
record. I can find the song on the radio. Anyway, I
can't play it. I have no phonograph."

He was quiet again for at least another minute and
then he said, "Another thing you should know about
me—I'm Jewish, the spoiled brat, first son of educated,
affluent, and liberal parents. Many people resent me for
having avoided the draft by going to college. Never
mind that I do have flat feet. I can't imagine not having
a phonograph. I have my own in my room that I can
play anytime."

Lenny's face was flushed by the end of his
outburst. What did anyone say to all that? I blurted out
my first reaction.

"I'm Catholic. Does that bother you?"

He laughed and squeezed my hand.

"No, not at all. I was taught to value the person,
not the color of his skin or his religion. I love my
parents. They're super, especially my mother. I'm sorry
I sounded so strident, but I know that who I am
bothers some people. And sometimes I can't help
feeling guilty that I have so much."

"Yes, I should resent you. You're so blessed. But
I've never thought about things like you're talking
about—what kind of person I am, what kind you are. I
love my parents, too, and they love me, but we don't say
it to each other. I don't know why. They think it's a
waste of time to talk about it."

"Actually, we hardly talk much about such things, either. We take it for granted we all love each other and hug and kiss a lot. Many people are uncomfortable expressing emotions, but not my family. I wonder sometimes if it's because their ancestors suffered much in Europe and they could endure suffering better if they shared it."

"Do you know your family's history?"

"Only, in general. You and I have one thing in common. My great-great-grandparents—I think that's who they are—immigrated to this country from Germany in the late 1800s. My parents told us their ancestors had to move around. They lived in countries like Czechoslovakia and probably even Poland, before settling in Germany. Maybe, it wasn't called Germany at the time."

"I think mine lived in an area that's now part of Poland. I remember from European history class that present Poland didn't exist as a state until the late 1800s."

I was thrilled to know Lenny and I had more in common than I thought. He had always seemed so different from me and, maybe, that was partly why I was attracted to him. Having some shared history drew me even closer to him.

He picked up the record off the table and waved it back and forth.

"I bet you can convince your aunt to play this on her stereo. If not, I bet I can convince her."

I smiled. I bet he could, too. My aunt liked him. It
was obvious in the way she talked to him. And I liked
Lenny; maybe, I even loved him.

VIII. Courtship

When Lenny took me home from the soda fountain on our first two Fridays out, I had asked him to let me off on another street a block or two from Aunt Jola's house. I wasn't ready for anyone to know I was going out with him. The third afternoon, he dropped me off directly in front of her house.

"Why don't I come in with you? I'd like to see how your aunt's doing."

I hesitated, worried that my aunt would disapprove of my going out with Lenny. But I had to explain to her how I got the record, if I wanted to listen to it. I had planned to say Lenny lent it to me and hoped she wouldn't ask why. But what if she did? Besides, I felt so unsure of myself that I knew I'd need someone's advice sooner or later and I could only ask Aunt Jola.

"Okay. I'm sure she'll be glad to see you."

But, I didn't have to explain anything to my aunt. She understood right away when she saw us standing at her doorsteps. She frowned at me, then Lenny, and with a sweep of her hand, led us into her house.

"I should have known you, young people, would go ahead and do what you want, never mind what we, old people, say."

Lenny ignored her remark. "How are you feeling, Aunt Jola?"

"Tired, sleepy, woozy. It's those medications they're giving me. I can't do many things I used to do. The nurse keeps reassuring me I'll get back to normal but it's taking a while. The doctor told me to wait about another month before asking my pupils to come back for their lessons. So, I'm irritable and, if I snap at you, don't take it personally."

She glanced my way. "Agnes is used to my moods. I can be foul sometimes, but she's a patient one and loves me, anyway. Don't you, my pet?"

I merely smiled, somewhat annoyed at her tone. She was back to treating me like a child.

Lenny arched an eyebrow at me. He understood what I had to put up with. To Aunt Jola, he flashed a reassuring smile.

"You do get back to normal. My grandmother did. Actually, you're looking good, like you did before the hospital. And if I look as good as you do when I'm old, then I won't mind aging."

I saw Aunt Jola wince, probably at Lenny's remark about being old like his grandmother. But, she smiled.

"You say I look good, huh? Maybe, that new regimen they've put me on is helping."

She gave him a warm seductive smile, as she sashayed into the living room. We followed her there.

"It's nice of you to come by and ask about me, even if you may be lying."

"Me? Lie? I always call it like I see it," Lenny said with a feigned scowl.

My aunt smiled at Lenny again, placed her hand on his elbow, and led us to the sofa.

"Sit down, Lenny, and tell me what you two have been up to." She sat down next to him.

To me, she said, "Agnes, can you get us some soda? Get me one of those awful diet ones."

She spoke to me, but her gaze didn't stray away from Lenny.

"Let me help you, Agnes," Lenny said, rising from the sofa.

Aunt Jola grabbed his hand and pulled him back down. "Stay. I want to know how you got this young woman to go out with you."

Lenny shrugged his shoulders. He winked and smiled at me.

When I came back with a tray of glasses, soda, and ice in Aunt Jola's special bucket, Lenny was describing the drugstore soda fountain and its lively atmosphere. I laid the tray on the coffee table and poured the soda. I handed the two their filled glasses.

I sat down on a chair across from them. I sipped my soda and watched Aunt Jola. I was anxious, searching for signs that she disapproved of my going out with Lenny. She turned to me and regarded me for a minute.

"I can't believe you've never been to a soda fountain. Your parents haven't taken you to one?"

My aunt obviously didn't think it wrong—my dating Lenny. I relaxed, smiling, ready to be charitable toward my parents.

I said, "I guess it never occurred to them to take me. And, these last eight years, I spent my free time practicing piano."

"True. But now, I wish I'd spent a little time showing you other things—fun things. There's more to life than the piano."

"It's not your responsibility, Aunt Jola."

"No, maybe not. But nobody else took it on."

She gazed at me, a frown forming on her forehead.

"Maybe I shouldn't be saying this. But why the heck not? I'm sick and I could die from this illness. I think that entitles me to say anything I want."

I perked up, eager to hear what prompted her dramatic words. But she paused and I worried for some moments that she might have sudden qualms about what she meant to say. I'd seen her keyed up before, but the next moment she'd lost interest.

"Your parents are such puritans. Your mother, especially. Afraid of enjoying herself. Afraid of life. That's not a happy atmosphere for bringing up children."

I realized when she finally spoke that she was afraid to hurt me. She thought the truth was so momentous that, if I heard her say it, my relationship with my parents could worsen.

My aunt's rant shocked me a bit, at first, and it made me uneasy. But I smiled, feeling both consternated and amused. My gaze flitted between Aunt Jola and Lenny. Then, I laughed. I wasn't sure why. Maybe, I was embarrassed.

Whatever the reason, my laughter lightened everyone's mood. Aunt Jola and Lenny started to laugh, too.

"Is that all, Aunt Jola? It's not a crime to be Puritan, is it?"

Lenny said, "No. Anyway, they can't be Puritans. Not strictly speaking. You're Catholic, right?"

We gaped at him, puzzled.

"Well, you see, the Puritans were originally a group who broke off from a Protestant church. Now, people use the word to mean something else that's got nothing to do with religion. The original Puritans were probably not prudish or moralistic."

"Ohhh."

Aunt Jola and I stared at each other and shrugged.

She said, "Well, anyway, that's off my chest. Don't get me wrong. I love my niece, Agnes's mother. I took care of her on that long voyage from Poland. We also shared a bed for two years after we got here. But she exasperates me sometimes. She's more old-fashioned and rigid than me and I'm at least ten years older."

Aunt Jola reached over and touched my hand.

"I don't think you'll be like your mother, Agnes, not with that fire you have for your instrument. And I sense love in the air. I do get a thrill watching young love. Such passion. Maybe, Ania would be different if she experienced that."

Aunt Jola smiled mischievously.

"We're not going steady, Aunt Jola. We've gone out three times to the same place, after school. That's all. We're testing the waters, so to speak."

"I see. You, maybe, are getting your feet wet, but I bet that's not true for Lenny. Is it, Lenny?"

"If you're asking if have I gone steady before, you're right, Aunt Jola. A few times, in high school, and I've gone out on dates at the university. All for fun."

"Ah, yes. Fun. Nothing serious, then. Good. Keep it that way. Agnes is only sixteen."

I wanted to protest again, tell my aunt Lenny knew how old I was, and she had no business dictating how he should treat me. I also wanted to shout: *Look at me. I'm not a child anymore. A man—good-looking, smart, wonderful—could not get me out of his head. Me— small, thin, awkward.*

But I heeded Mama's lessons about respect for my elders.

Lenny winked at me. He must have sensed my irritation. "It'd be fun showing Agnes all the nice places in the city. You haven't gone much beyond this neighborhood, have you, Agnes?"

I shook my head.

"Maybe I could take you, or both you and Aunt Jola, to a concert at Heinz Hall when the season starts."

"You're being sly, young man. I know I'm just the passport and the excuse for you to take her out in the evening, but I'm game. I'm willing to put up with a lot to go to a concert."

She turned to me. "I can help advance the course of young love. To a point."

I had yet to find out what she meant by "to a point." That afternoon, I was content to be grateful. She didn't object to my seeing Lenny and didn't mind being used as an excuse when I went out with him. It was more than I had hoped for.

Later that night, I lay awake, thinking back on my aunt's rant about my "puritanical" parents. The incident bothered me and I wanted to understand why. I knew I needed relief from how tense I felt over Aunt Jola's "truth," but that alone wouldn't have made me laugh. I laughed because my aunt's outburst embarrassed me and Lenny was there. I didn't want him to think my parents were dour and harsh. He seemed embarrassed, too, maybe, for me and my parents—for that, I liked him even more.

I should have defended my parents from my aunt's criticism but I didn't know how. The truth was, I saw them that way, as well. And yet, I was sure they loved me and were doing their best. But, I also saw then how limited their best was.

*****

Lenny and Aunt Jola were both true to their words. He took me to different places around the city— places so unfamiliar that I felt like a tourist, seeing the city I was born in for the very first time. He also dropped me off now at her house, stopping by sometimes to talk to her. If he and I had previously agreed to stay out later than usual, we told her about it.

We sought Aunt Jola's complicity and she always found some excuse to give my mother for why I was late. On my first weekend out with Lenny, we went to the first museum I ever visited. Aunt Jola told my mother she was taking me to it, to thank me for helping her with household chores while she was recovering.

My mother, usually lacking curiosity, nodded her assent. Aunt Jola actually stayed home, but played the part of being out for the day very well. She locked up her house, didn't answer her phone, and didn't open her door to anyone until Lenny dropped me off in the evening.

Days proceeded in much the same way for a few months, until the evening Lenny took me and Aunt Jola to a concert, as he had promised. It was my first concert and my first night out.

Aunt Jola told my mother one of her pupils gave her tickets to the concert and she would like to take me to it.

Mama asked, "Does she need a formal dress for this fancy evening?"

"I'd want one, if it were me. I told her I'd help her dress, put a little lipstick on her, do her hair. With a new dress, she'd feel special. You don't mind, do you? She's getting to be quite a lovely young woman, one any mother can be proud of."

"Yes, I know."

My aunt was sure Mama meant "yes." She was right.

Two days before the concert, my mother presented me a pretty blue dress. She held it up against my figure.

"The color goes well with your hair and your eyes."

I nearly burst into tears. I wanted to hug her, but I knew she was uncomfortable with close physical contact. I took her hand and kissed it.

With a new dress on a hanger, protected in a plastic bag, I walked to my aunt's house, two hours before Lenny came to pick us up. Before I could put the dress on, Aunt Jola painted my face with her creams, pencils, and brushes, and mercilessly pulled and pinned my hair up.

When she was done, I peeked at my reflection in the mirror. My aunt had a subtle hand. Those pencils and brushes didn't make obvious marks, except for my pinker lips, lusher lashes, and the sophisticated young lady standing before me.

My aunt grinned broadly. "Hello, beautiful!"

When Lenny came, he whistled and ogled us both with obvious admiration.

"How lucky can one man get? I'll have the two most stunning women hanging on my arms this evening."

The concert featured a young violinist who walked to the stage on his crutches. I was so riveted by his music that everything around me faded. I could feel the notes vibrating through my body. My eyes were moist when the second movement, a wrenching, but hopeful adagio, came to a close.

A break in the program followed the violin concerto. But the music continued to play in my head.

Aunt Jola whispered in my ear, "I need to go to the bathroom. Are you coming?"

I shook my head. I had to sit quietly for a little while.

"How about you, Lenny?"

He chuckled. "I don't think they have unisex bathrooms here."

"Huh?"

"No, Aunt Jola, I think I'll keep Agnes company."

She got up, scowling, murmuring something about the stamina of youth.

Lenny and I stayed in our seats. I smiled gratefully at him.

"Thank you for taking me to this concert. It's wonderful and the violinist is so good."

He placed his arm around my shoulders, gathered me closer and pressed his lips lightly on mine. My first kiss. I had wondered how it was going to be and when.

"Did you mind that?"

"No. It's nice. But my aunt will be back any minute now."

"You look like a dream tonight. I think I'm falling in love with you," he whispered before he released me.

His arm around me had felt possessive. He had put an arm around my shoulders before, to lead me into or out of a room or protect me from a rushing crowd. I had not interpreted it as anything romantic, although I did tingle when he first put his arm around me. This time was different.

I was giddy at the thought that Lenny was falling in love with me. But I was scared, too. I'd been excited when I realized I had a crush on him, and I wanted so

much to be with him. How different was true love
between a man and a woman?

I assumed that it was more serious than a crush,
and could lead to a lifetime spent together. And I
wasn't so naïve that I didn't know what could happen
between a man and a woman when they were alone in a
room together. I started learning about it in my
childhood.

Through the thin walls in our apartment, I could
hear my parents in their bedroom when they talked or
went about their habitual preparations for bed.
Moaning from their room had awakened me one night.
I was six and I got scared. I called out to my mother,
but she didn't come. I called out a few more times and
still got no answer.

I thought about running to the door, but I was too
scared that some monster might be in the hallway. So, I
curled myself up into a ball and hid under my blanket. I
fell asleep under the covers.

When I woke up in the morning, the blanket had
been pulled down to my neck. My mother had come in
the night to check on me. She had tucked the blanket
under my chin.

The following nights, I stayed awake to listen for
those sounds, but a long time passed before I heard
them again. I didn't call out to my mother then, but I
did hide under my covers. In the morning, they had
been drawn down to my neck. In junior high, I learned
from classmates what those moaning sounds meant.

I couldn't concentrate on the concert after that
kiss. The young violinist came back to play an even

longer piece. The audience gave him a standing ovation
that must have lasted more than ten minutes.

My aunt was clapping like a prim lady in her seat,
but her eyes shone and she stopped several times to
carefully dab her eyes with one of her fancy
handkerchiefs. When we all stood up to leave, she
kissed Lenny on the cheek.

"Thank you."

"My pleasure. I knew you ladies would love it. But
concerts make me hungry so the least you could do to
show your appreciation is to allow me to take you to my
favorite drive-in. I have a hankering for a milkshake."

"Well, in that case, what are we waiting for?" My
aunt hooked her hand on Lenny's arm.

He clasped my hand with his free one and pulled
me closer to him. I suspected the milkshake was an
excuse for us to be together longer.

In the car, Lenny and I sat in front, my aunt in the
back. At the drive-in, he held my hand, resting
between us on the seat. Every so often, he rubbed his
thumb against my palm, a gesture both soothing and
intimate. My heart was aflutter but I sat rigid and
silent. I couldn't show any visible reaction, afraid I'd
arouse my aunt's suspicions.

From the drive-in, he dropped me off first. My
aunt walked me to my house and we waited on the
front porch until my mother opened the door.

"Well, here she is. Back, safe and sound"

Without waiting for an answer, Aunt Jola left.

My mother squinted her eyes, searching the street. I grabbed Mama's elbow to lead her back up the stairs, but she shook my hand off.

"Let's go in. It's cold out here," I said.

I was concerned she might recognize Lenny's car. She'd been in it once when we picked Aunt Jola up at the hospital. I dreaded for her to become suspicious. She'd put an end to my seeing Lenny, and I still had to discover where that first kiss would lead to.

I walked into the house, but Mama didn't come in until minutes later. She followed me to my bedroom.

"How did you get back? Was there someone else with you? Is your aunt seeing someone?"

"No, Mama. We took a cab."

I felt a nip of guilt for my answer. I was growing adept at blurting out little lies. But I quickly justified myself with the thought that Aunt Jola was lying, too. Besides, my mother was unlikely to understand this strong attraction I felt for Lenny.

"That wasn't a cab she got into. It had no light on top. Your Aunt Jola should be careful. She could be easy prey."

"She's not so rich that they'd go after her for her money."

"No, but she's more than comfortable and that's enough for some men. And she's still quite attractive for her age."

IX. Falling

Lenny is in love with me, I told myself several times before reality sank in. Now, I could admit to myself that my crush on him had grown into something bigger. After the night of the concert, I became more eager to be with him and more restless when I didn't see him.

I pushed aside my concern that my parents would find out about us. If they still thought I was a young girl under their protection and control, they wouldn't see me as a grown woman and were less likely to suspect I was seeing someone.

Before the concert, Lenny and I saw each other on Fridays and occasional weekends. The rest of my weekday afternoons, I adhered to my schedule, spending after-school hours at my aunt's house, learning new pieces and practicing.

My life changed again the Wednesday following the concert. I saw Lenny, in his car, parked among others waiting to pick up students at the end of the school day.

I got into the front passenger seat and we drove away.

"What's up? Do you suddenly have an appetite for ice cream soda?"

He laughed and caressed my left cheek.

"No I suddenly had an appetite for feasting on the sight of your face, especially your blue eyes."

I sucked my breath into my mouth. I was getting flushed at his gaze, his voice, and his touch.

He turned his attention back to the road. He added in a lower voice, "Your kissable lips, too."

I fought the urge to touch my lips with my fingertips. I felt myself trembling, remembering that first kiss. It occurred to me, then, that everyone got her first romantic kiss only once in her life. She could later get a first kiss from another lover, but it wouldn't be the same. That very first one had special significance and if it was from someone she loved, she'd never ever forget it.

Lenny and I didn't go to the soda fountain that afternoon.

"Would you object if I took you to my dorm room instead?"

"You're not planning to take advantage of me, are you? I'm old-fashioned, you know. I'm saving myself for the man I marry."

I had to say something and that line, which I heard in a film or read in a book, sounded impressive. But I wasn't sure I meant it. I had never thought of what marriage was all about.

Lenny burst into a booming laugh.

"I wish I'd seen your face when you said that. But, no, I don't intend to take advantage of you. I promised your aunt I'll behave, at least until you're old enough, although I don't know when that is. I wanted some quiet time alone with you. That's all. The crowd at the soda fountain is too much for me on a Wednesday afternoon. I usually spend it studying at the library."

So, we went to his dorm room. In the lobby and along the hallway, he raised a hand to greet some people, obviously all students. I was impressed by how many acquaintances and friends he had. I felt shy and self-conscious. I didn't want them to imagine we were going to his room to neck. But I couldn't help wondering how many girls Lenny had taken to his room precisely for that. I assumed college students— with all the freedom they had—often did that.

The room had two beds and two desks. Lenny shared it with another student, who had classes and wasn't expected back until six o'clock. I never met him, even once, while I knew Lenny.

Lenny took out his record collection and told me to pick one to play. He had many classical albums, but half his records were pop tunes I was unfamiliar with. Two or three albums caught my eye, but I chose one that bore the song he first played on the jukebox. Since I liked that song, I would probably like others on the album. Lenny was pleased at my selection.

"Did you know this is my favorite album? For now, at least. There's always something new, you know. I actually thought you might pick classical music."

"If modern songs are all like *American Pie*, I wanna listen to more. I'm sure I'd like them, too."

"You can listen to the other records next time you come. I have the best ones. We'll get you listening and swinging to pop music in no time at all."

As he turned on his stereo, I looked around for a place to sit and found nothing but hard desk chairs. Lenny nudged me by the elbow toward his bed and we climbed on top of it as the album began to spin. He put pillows behind us and we sat, leaning our heads and backs against the wall. I folded my legs, and he extended his out and down to the floor. We listened without saying a word. The songs took more than a half-hour to play.

Halfway through the second song, Lenny reached over for my right hand. I stiffened, but his hand was so warm and soft and his gesture so natural that I let go. But when he spread my palm on his thigh, his hand on mine, I couldn't suppress a gasp. I glanced up at him. He had not noticed my reaction. His eyes were closed and he seemed lost in the music.

I told myself to relax, but my heart was beating fast and my limbs had turned to jelly. It hit me then that I was alone in a man's room, with my hand resting on his hard thigh. Would Aunt Jola disapprove?

Mama would, in the silent reproachful way she could keep up for days. She would impose other restrictions on me, forbid me to go to Aunt Jola's. That would be punishing. My aunt was like a lifeline to me and I couldn't imagine no longer seeing her.

For an instant, I panicked and nearly jumped from the bed to go home right away to Aunt Jola's. I took a few deep breaths and the feeling passed.

My desire to be with Lenny was stronger than my worries about my mother and my aunt, and I couldn't believe I was doing something wrong. Being with him

felt good. Maybe not as good as when I flawlessly
played a favorite piece on the piano, but it came a close
second. It was also quite different from my affection for
my aunt.

I got over the urge to flee, but in its place, a
stronger urge took over and nearly overwhelmed me. I
imagined running my hand slowly along Lenny's thigh,
exploring its shape, kneading the muscles in it,
caressing the skin. And, I would watch how he reacted.
I closed my eyes tight, and did nothing more than lock
those thoughts deep in my brain.

When the record was over, Lenny released my
hand. He bounced up from the bed.

"Let's go. I have to study and you have piano
lessons."

He was scowling and his skin was flushed.

I was taken aback. We'd been out later, before that
afternoon. I expected to play more records, stay
another hour.

But I also had homework. So, I dragged myself off
the bed and grabbed my schoolbag without a word.

He stopped his car a block from Aunt Jola's house.
Before I could get out, he gathered me in his arms and
kissed me, a deeper, longer kiss than the first. Then, he
reached past me and pushed the door open.

"I'll see you on Friday," he said, in a tone more like
a question.

He left me with a vague sense that something had
gone wrong. But my head was in a daze and I couldn't
think too clearly. I picked up my bag on the car floor
and swung one shaky leg, then the other, out on the

sidewalk. I couldn't say anything or look at Lenny. I banged his door shut without meaning to.

I somehow made it to my aunt's front porch on shaky legs, about the time he drove away.

Strands of hair had fallen loose from my barrette and on my face. I tucked them away, composed my mouth into a smile, and rang the doorbell. My aunt was frowning when she opened the door.

"You're late today. Anything happened at school?"

I shook my head as I entered. She watched me, her eyes curious, and I didn't dare raise mine to hers. Not that I felt guilty about being kissed. My Catholic conscience was not that strong. But I was conscious that I got excited from the kiss. My heart fluttered, I had to catch my breath, and warmth swept through the center of my body down to my limbs. I was afraid she'd see all that in my eyes.

My aunt did see through me.

"Were you with Lenny today?"

I didn't lie. There was no point. I nodded.

"Well, it was bound to happen. I think that boy is in love with you. Has been for some time. I told him to go easy and, for the most part, I think he's tried."

"Oh, Aunt Jola, do you really think he loves me? But why?"

"Why? Who knows why people fall in love? I can tell you what might have attracted him to you."

"Then, tell me. This is all new to me. If I love him back, I'd like to know why he loves me."

"Do you love him, too? I suspect you do but I can't be sure."

"If I like being with him more than anything, even more than playing the piano, is that love?"

"It's at least the beginning."

"I see. But I gotta know why he loves me. Maybe, that'll push me one way or the other."

"You're a cautious one. Maybe, that's good. I know he's thrilled that you have a passion for music. Lenny is an artistic soul and that speaks to him. And, of course, because you're beautiful."

"You really think I'm beautiful?"

"Come, see for yourself."

She took my hand and led me to a mirror in her living room. She released my hair from its barrette and it tumbled in golden waves on my shoulders and halfway down my back.

"Many women spend real money for hair that color and that thick. Throw in your clear blue eyes, ivory skin, and that innocent glow of youth and many men would grovel at your feet."

"Do I look innocent?"

"Yeah, you do. Maybe, it helps that you don't pay your looks much attention, don't wear make-up except at concerts. But you *are* innocent, aren't you? You haven't gone to bed with him, have you?"

"No, no. But why is innocent attractive?"

"Who knows? Some men like to be the one to initiate you into the art of love. I suppose it feeds their ego. Fortunately, most men aren't that way. Maybe some young men are less intimidated by innocent girls, especially if they themselves don't have much experience. But I don't think Lenny's like that."

"What's Lenny like, Aunt Jola?"

"Oh, child, you're asking too many questions. Don't you know? Anyway, it doesn't matter what I think. It's what you think of him that does."

"I see."

"Well, of course, if he's bad, I'll tell you not to go out with him and, if you don't listen to me, I'll tell your mother."

We laughed at that. We had both learned to regard my mother with some sense of humor, at least, occasionally.

"One day, you'll be tempted and when that happens, make sure you're protected. They teach you things like that in school, don't they?"

I nodded, blushing profusely. I wished I could ask her what it was like, how she found it, what I could expect, but I was too embarrassed.

Lenny and I began spending more time together. My aunt knew, but I didn't tell her when and how and she didn't ask me. I devoted fewer hours to the piano, which I justified by telling myself my dreams had been crushed long ago. I was past sadness over it and being with Lenny helped. I was content, for now, to experience falling in love.

Still, in the back of my mind lurked the unhappy thought that I had to seek my future somewhere other than music. Lenny might be in that future. Or, he might not.

*****

Wednesday afternoons in Lenny's dorm room became part of our routine. You could guess what happened after that second kiss and you would be right. Shortly after my seventeenth birthday, I lost my virginity. In his dorm room, on a Wednesday afternoon.

Years later, I could hardly remember how it happened. Like a first kiss, it could never be repeated and I would have liked to have good memories. I could recall my very first kiss quite vividly—the setting, the sounds, Lenny's soft, tender lips. So, why was it a blur—that first time he made love to me?

I did know I was eager and excited in the beginning despite my ignorance, but I got scared when Lenny undid the buttons on my shirt. I wanted to keep my clothes on and stop him from groping me all over. In the end, curiosity and defiance of all those little lessons from my mother overcame my inhibitions.

I kept my eyes closed the whole time. After I felt Lenny quiver and say, "I love you," it was over. The experience was bewildering.

Did I expect magic? Actually, I didn't know what to expect. All I really knew about lovemaking was the little hinted at in sex education classes, which focused on contraception.

If any of my girlfriends had done it, they weren't talking. A few had boyfriends and they kissed out in the open, when teachers weren't around. When some girl got pregnant, then we were sure she had gone all the way. One or two girls were rumored to "give it out freely." They were popular with boys. Some girls felt contempt for them, but in the era of sexual freedom and women's liberation, most of us didn't care.

My experience got better as I grew less anxious and could concentrate on momentary sensations. I had to admit it was more than pleasant, and I was willing to do it as much as Lenny did.

We were deeply in love. How else were we to explain the tender moments; the incredible feeling of floating in the clouds when we were together; the delicious sensations in my body thinking about him; the promises of a world beyond my current existence?

But if love was what had me in its grip, what was passion? How could it possibly be better?

Lenny was solicitous and affectionate. He was a girl's dream come true and he had chosen me. He showered me with gifts, mostly little jewelry pieces I could easily hide. They were tokens—according to him—of his love and gratitude for what we had together.

I finally felt myself liberated and living within my time. I realized later that I had been living in the era my parents had grown up in, dealing with residual insecurities from their unfortunate childhood.

My world grew with Lenny. He exposed me to places, things, people and ideas about which I knew very little. It was a sign of my naiveté that I thought life could only get better; that my aunt would not betray me to my mother if she discovered I was no longer innocent; that my parents would never know about Lenny until I was old enough to do as I pleased, less than a year away.

I wasn't so naïve to think Lenny would propose, and as my world grew, I learned I wasn't ready to settle down. He had only shown me glimpses of life as he saw it and I wanted to experience it in more depth. But as the person who taught me how to love and as my first love, he would always be a part of me. If things had been different, we might have married when we were both ready, and spent our lives together.

Incidents that could catalyze a change in the course of a life could be ordinary and not momentous at all. Sometimes you wouldn't even realize they were important until you looked back. That was how a big change in my life began—with a small talk about jewelry.

X. Falling Out

Routines ruled our home. They had varied little ever since I could remember. I didn't hate them. They had been reassuring while I was growing up, and when I was older, they were actually relaxing. One routine that never changed was dinner at seven o'clock, after which my mother and I cleared the table and washed dishes while my father read his paper.

Often, Mama and I went about our chores in silence, but every once in a while, she got curious about something and would start a conversation, as she did one evening.

"Your aunt was wearing some jewelry today that I've never seen before."

I shrugged. "So, she bought a new one. She can spend her money as she likes."

"I know, except that your aunt will spend thousands on a grand piano—"

"And, she did," I interrupted her impatiently.

"—but she has not bought jewelry since she came to live here. Her husband gave her so much and she didn't need anymore. I've seen them all. She boasted about them to me when she lived with us for two months. She told me not too long ago, she was going to leave them all to you."

"She's never told me that. Anyway, I don't wear jewelry much. I really don't have any, just a few trinkets bought with savings from my allowance."

I didn't tell my mother about the few little "trinkets" Lenny gave me. She had already seen me wear one, a little piano pin of white gold she assumed was tin.

"She means to give them to you."

"I've only seen Aunt Jola wear her wedding ring and earrings, three or four different ones. I wasn't aware she had more."

"She must have about two dozen earrings. That's all she showed me. No necklaces or bracelets."

My mother threw me a quick glance.

"You'd better learn to love earrings, if you're to inherit."

I heard mirth in her voice, which drew my curiosity. She was smiling broadly, her eyes amused—a rare expression for her. I saw then that she was beautiful. She had delicate, regular features, but I only used to notice the persistent scowl, the mouth pressed tight, and the deep lines they caused on her brow and around her mouth. Many years later when Elise was five, I realized that, like me, she inherited Mama's mouth. Mama pursed hers to hide how sensuous they were.

I grinned back at Mama, happy to share her amusement.

"I'd better get my ears pierced, then. I hope her new jewelry is not another pair of earrings, or I'll need several piercings."

My mother actually chuckled.

"No, it's a tiny pin she wears on her lapel. It has this glitter you couldn't miss so I made a remark about it. She said, 'Oh, this. A tiny trinket I picked up at the dime store. I don't know why, but I liked it right away.' But it's no dime store trinket. I'm sure it's diamond."

"Okay, so it's diamond. She can afford it."

"Yes, she can, but I think someone gave it to her."

"Maybe, it's a gift from the parents of one of her pupils; to show how much they appreciate her teaching."

"A diamond? I don't think so."

"She bought it, then, like I thought."

"I think someone else did give it to her. I asked you once if she's seeing someone. Well, I think she is."

I shrugged my shoulders again. The dishes were all dried and put away so I wiped my hands on my apron and took it off.

"Homework," I said.

I didn't wait to find out if she had something more to say. For me, that ended the talk about Aunt Jola's jewelry. My mother expected me to share with her what she thought I knew. But there was nothing to tell and even if there were, Aunt Jola could tell Mama what she wanted her to know. I would respect anyone's wish to keep something to herself.

I had almost forgotten that conversation when two weeks later, while doing dishes, Mama brought it up again.

"Now, I'm pretty sure your aunt has a new man."

"So? She's free. She's not married and, like you said, she's still quite attractive."

"So, you haven't met or seen him?"

"No. Maybe, he comes at night after my piano practice. Or, maybe, he comes on weekends. I'm usually home then except when Aunt Jola and I go somewhere together."

Going somewhere on a weekend with my aunt was the excuse I used to give my mother when I saw Lenny on a Saturday. In fact, my aunt and I never went anywhere by ourselves.

My mother said, "He comes earlier. Her next-door neighbor tells me that, about twice a week, there's this car—the same one all the time—that's parked by her house in late afternoon. Come to think of it, it would be about the time before you come home from her place. So, you ought to have seen him."

"Well, I haven't. Maybe he times his coming to just after I leave. They probably wanna be alone."

I knew, for sure my mother was talking about Lenny's car. But I wasn't about to tell her.

"How do you know it's a man?"

"The neighbor saw him once or twice."

I started to worry at that point. If Mama continued nosing around Aunt Jola's house, it might not take long before she found out about me and Lenny.

That night, I lay awake thinking about whether I should come clean and tell my mother about Lenny. But I needed someone with whom I could share confidences or have a girl-to-girl talk like I did with Aunt Jola. Confidences required trust and, at the very

least, tolerance. Acceptance was better. But Mama
would be judgmental and I couldn't trust her to
understand my feelings.

I never told my mother about Lenny. In nine more
months, I was going to be eighteen—to me, a magic
age, the age I would be free—and I was impatient to
reach it.

*****

Two months later, my mother found out I was
seeing someone. Not from me, but from Aunt Jola. We
were cleaning up after dinner, several nights before
everything came to a head.

"You're right. That man goes to your aunt's house
at night. The neighbor saw the car there on
Wednesday night and it stayed more than an hour after
midnight."

I cast her a quick, uneasy glance. I saw Lenny on
Wednesday but he dropped me off at Aunt Jola's at the
usual time in late afternoon. He left after a short banter
with Aunt Jola. If that was his car, what was he doing
there at midnight?

The following day, Saturday, I decided to go to
Aunt Jola's. My mother's little gossip had kept me
awake for about an hour the night before.

"What do I owe this visit to? Is Lenny coming? Are
you going out today and you forgot to tell me about it?"

"No, I'm not expecting him today. Are you?"

"No, of course not." Her voice was sharper and
louder than usual. "What makes you say that?"

"Mama gossips with your next-door neighbor, who saw his car here on Wednesday midnight."

"So, your mother was talking to my neighbors and snooping on me?"

"She got curious when she saw your new diamond pin. She thought a new boyfriend gave it to you."

Aunt Jola glared at me for what seemed like an endless minute. "I think I know who told her. We have two busybodies, but one lives three houses away so it couldn't be her. She's the nosier one, too."

"Well, was Lenny here that night?"

"He was, but it's not what they're thinking. He came to give me a check from his parents for his brother's lessons."

"Why did he come so late? Couldn't he have waited until the following day?"

"Ask him yourself," Aunt Jola answered irritably. "What he told me was he's had the check for more than a week but had forgotten it. That evening, he saw it in his wallet. He came right away so he wouldn't forget it again. Contrary to that gossip who's filling your mother's head with ideas, he was here about twenty minutes."

I wanted to believe Aunt Jola. I owed her so much, so I let the matter go. We spent the rest of the afternoon playing rondos.

I was ready to forget what I thought was a minor episode that started with a small piece of jewelry. But it seemed to be growing into a sticky incident. Unlike me Aunt Jola was not about to let it go.

Besides cleaning up after dinner, Mama and I
shared another routine. We went to mass on Sundays
and, from there, to the supermarket. Since meeting
Lenny, I grew more casual about my religion, but I
continued going to church with my mother to pacify
her.

The Sunday after I confronted Aunt Jola about the
gossip her neighbor shared with Mama, she came to
our house shortly before noon. I opened the door to let
her in. Mama was unloading our grocery purchases on
the dining table.

"This is an unexpected pleasure. I'm about to start
making our Sunday dinner. Can you stay long enough
to join us?"

"Thank you for the invitation but I don't know if I
can stay. Can we talk, alone?"

Aunt Jola didn't smile. She wasn't pleased. Mama
hesitated. Maybe, she dreaded what Aunt Jola had to
say or, maybe, she didn't want to disrupt her routine.
But my mother glanced at her aunt's clenched jaw and
mouth pressed as tight as hers and knew she had no
choice.

"Agnieszka, can you start the roast, after you've
put things away? Wash the cabbage and an onion and
slice them thin."

She turned to Aunt Jola.

"Why don't we go to the front porch. We can close
the door to the house from there."

I was left alone, burning with curiosity. I could feel
the tension between them and I sensed that something
awful was about to happen.

*****

The apartment wasn't designed for privacy and the building was built cheaply. Its walls were thin enough that, if you talked low, a person in another room could still hear murmurs. You didn't need to raise your voice much for your conversation to be understood by the listener in another room. He might not hear every word, but he could fill in gaps. That afternoon, I listened as I started preparations for Sunday dinner.

"You've been spying on me. I don't like it. It's none of your business what I do," I heard my aunt say before my mother closed the door to the front porch.

Mama's answer was muffled, but I understood it.

"That goes for me, too. What I do is none of your business."

I strained to listen but I could only hear snippets. Even so, I could tell that their argument had quickly turned to being about me.

For some minutes, words came to me as a low buzz, too garbled for me to make out, but soon after, my mother's loud angry voice passed through the walls clearly.

"How dare you say that! I have done the best for my daughter. Is it my fault we can't afford to send her to an expensive music school? Is it my fault we're poor and I brought my child into poverty? I didn't want to have children because I knew we couldn't give them all they'd ask for. But I had Agnieszka and, like us, she'd have to make do with what we can afford."

"I offered to help her." My aunt's voice was also louder.

They were both growing angrier and their argument was headed for the worst. I felt my body tense up.

"You just want to keep us indebted to you."

"Ania, what's wrong with accepting help from people? What are you trying to prove?"

"Nothing. I'm not trying to prove anything. I'm trying my best to live without relying on anyone else. And that's what I'm teaching my daughter."

"You won't accept help even from me, your one existing older relative, your father's sister?"

"No, not even you. So, I would appreciate it if you stop interfering in Agnieszka's life."

"How am I interfering in her life? I helped your daughter recognize her talent. Without me, you couldn't have. Without me, she wouldn't have developed it."

"But you filled her head with ideas and, now, she can't seem to be happy with her lot. And, she's turned against me. She thinks I've killed her dreams. She will continue to blame me for that."

"You're keeping a beautiful, talented child shackled to your narrow hopeless world."

"My daughter is my business, not yours. My world is her world."

My own anger had grown to the point where I needed to vent it. I could no longer take their argument and I marched into the front porch. Neither my mother nor my aunt appeared to have seen me.

"She can stop coming to me, if she wants to."

"You know, she won't. She's closer to you than she is to me."

"That's it, isn't it? You're jealous of my influence on her. But, I don't think that's all. It doesn't explain why you're spying on me, why you go around talking to my neighbors about what I do."

"Stop it, you two," I said, calmly, although I was shaking.

They ignored me. My mother clenched her fists to control her trembling limbs.

"I didn't set out to ask your neighbors about you. It just happened. I went to your house once and you weren't there. Your neighbor was in her yard and when I walked past her she said you must be out, that there's a car that comes late afternoon about twice a week. So, I thought you must be seeing someone."

"So what if I do? That's my business."

"If you make my daughter your business, why can't I make you mine? We're family aren't we? I get concerned. You give out this message you're open and waiting. You have money. You're still attractive. Many men out there prey on lonely women like you."

"How dare you talk to me like that? What are you implying? Why don't you keep an eye on your daughter instead of snooping on me? I bet you don't know the half of what she does."

I stared, alarmed, at my aunt. After all these months being my ally, was she going to give me away?

"Stop it!" I shouted.

But they continued as if I wasn't there.

"That's my business." Mama's tone was softer. She was obviously dismayed by Aunt Jola's remark about me.

Aunt Jola noticed her hesitation and took advantage of it.

"You're curious about that car parked at my house all the time? That's her boyfriend's."

I was stunned, confused, and ready to cry. Aunt Jola had done it. She betrayed a confidence that she had reassured me was safe with her. How could she, after I trusted her?

Mama said, "It couldn't be. This man visits you after Agnieszka has already left."

"Your gossip apparently doesn't see everything."

"His car was parked by your house at midnight. Agnieszka's always at home then, so he was seeing you. And, for your information, I know Agnieszka is seeing a boy in school."

I stared in disbelief at my mother. Was she bluffing?

"But she's keeping it a secret from you while she tells me everything that's going on with her. Why?"

"None of your business."

"Then, butt out of mine. And start earning your daughter's trust so she doesn't have to lie and sneak away to see that boy."

"You really are vicious. I think you should leave."

"And you're pathetic and narrow-minded.

"And you're a snake."

"You're both pathetic. And I hate you both!" I shouted on top of my voice.

But neither cared how I felt. They continued to glare daggers at each other.

I realized, then, that theirs was a personal battle to be won against one another and no one else. And both used me—my confidence in them and what they knew about me—to gain advantage over the other.

I was about to run, get out of their lives forever—that was how bad I felt at the moment—but my father barged in, newspaper still in hand. He grasped my arm and restrained me from leaving.

"You can't talk to your aunt and mother that way. Apologize."

I glared at him, my eyes blazing with anger. He stared back at me, bewildered. Then, he glowered at my mother.

"What's going on here? Your voices were so loud. The neighbors probably heard you."

"How could you not know what's going on here?" I said, bitterly. I pulled my arm away and pried his hand off. Then I ran out of the house.

I kept running, oblivious to the tears and sweat that blurred my vision, unconcerned about curious eyes and where I was headed. I flew down the hill, every step taking me as far away and as fast as I could from the only family I knew.

Many blocks later, just before I reached the bustling city below, I slowed down and tried to catch my breath. I wiped my wet face with my hands and went toward Lenny's dorm. It was, at least, a place to go.

That afternoon, I learned turmoil. I was dazed, disillusioned. And, yes, I wallowed in self-pity. I became angrier. I saw that I was caught between two women of my own blood. Responsible adults I was supposed to be able to trust, to rely on. They had a kind of rivalry between them—maybe some resentment, jealousy, bitterness they had kept going for a long time. For selfish ends, each was using me to one-up or get back at the other. I had to escape. Forever.

My steps were bound for Lenny's dorm, although I dreaded seeing him. Mama's gossip about him and my aunt echoed in my head. What was he really doing at her house at midnight? I could not imagine them being intimate. She was old enough to be his grandmother. Still, I had to admit it was odd that he visited her at midnight.

I had to find out the truth and soon. This seemed a good time to do so. What was one more confrontation? I searched for a phone booth.

XI. Leaving

The phone rang six times before someone picked it up.

"Hello."

I nearly burst out crying, hearing Lenny's voice, and I couldn't answer right away. I was overcome with relief to find I still had him. He was still there for me. When I ran away from my house, it seemed I lost everyone I cared for, or who cared for me. I had no one, and it scared me.

What I needed most, at that moment, was to talk to someone, to unburden myself and be assured he would listen without judging me. Lenny would, and he was all I had left. I pushed questions about his midnight visit to my aunt to the back of my head.

"Hello? Is someone there? I hear you panting, so please speak up."

"Hello, Lenny, it's me." My voice trembled, despite my effort to control it.

"Agnes! What's wrong? Have you been crying? Where are you?"

"In a phone booth."

I squinted my eyes at the sign on the street and told him what it was.

"That's about a mile away. Stay right there. I'll come get you. I should be there in five minutes."

Ten minutes later, we sat in his car as I related what happened. He let me talk, uninterrupted, his eyes brimming with sympathy. I couldn't bring up the midnight visit.

"I can't go back home. I don't wanna go back home."

"Well, I can get you a cheap hotel room near campus, for a day or two, until you feel better. I'm sure they'll be looking for you." He didn't offer any advice or persuade me to return.

"I don't want them to find me."

"If they don't find you right away, they'll call the police for help. So, I think they'll find you. Eventually."

"You won't tell my parents or Aunt Jola I'm here, will you?"

"No. I won't contact them. I promise. But I may be the first one they'll call and I'll have to tell them, then."

I scowled at him. I hated to hear him say that. The feeling that I was all alone and had no one I could turn to haunted me once again.

Lenny seemed to have read my mind.

"You need time to cool off. Anyway, you may decide to return home soon."

"No, never!"

"Give yourself time. When you feel better, you'll probably change your mind and go back."

"Isn't there a place I could go to and disappear?"

"There may be, but why would you do that? Your life is just beginning."

"I don't feel that way. I lost my dream and now I've also lost people I can trust, I should trust."

"You haven't lost them. I'm sure they'll want you back."

"But maybe, I don't want them back. I'm there for their own selfish reasons. Nothing more."

Lenny ignored my bitter words. He smiled, in his most charming way.

"I'm starved. Have you had dinner? I bet you're hungry, too. I have a hankering for fish and chips."

I was hungry. I had not eaten since a light breakfast of doughnut and coffee and he and I both liked fish and chips. But I shook my head.

"You have to be, if you ran all the way here. And crying saps energy."

He was teasing now, but I remained silent.

"Are you determined to make me beg for my food? Can you pick me up if I collapse here at your feet?"

I couldn't help smiling, then. Half an hour later, we were at the drive-in restaurant where we often got fish and chips.

Lenny drank the last drop of his soda and peeked at his watch.

"They may be looking for you about now. Your aunt has my phone number at the dorm. I wonder if they called."

Mentioning my aunt reminded me of the midnight visit, which I wasn't ready to confront. I had more immediate problems.

"I told you I'm not going home."

"I know. We'll check you into a hotel, for now. But aren't you concerned they'd be worried sick?"

"Let them. Maybe, they'll really think about me, for once, instead of what they can use me for."

In Lenny's car, on the way to the hotel, I began to shake.

"I haven't stayed in a hotel before. I haven't been on my own."

"Are you scared?"

"Yes. I was angry and frustrated when I ran out. But now, I'm frightened. I've never spent a night alone in a strange hotel."

"I can take you home, if you prefer."

"No! No way am I going back."

"If I had no roommate, I could have smuggled you into the dorm. It's forbidden, but I know it happens a lot and Resident Counselors tolerate it, if it's just for a day."

"Can't you stay with me?"

"We're not married and you're still technically a minor. I could go to jail."

Lenny paused and thought for a moment. Then, he grinned. "But I can smuggle myself into your room. It's actually easy to do in a hotel. The management is more likely to ignore it."

"I don't have a change of clothes."

"Go to bed without them. I can lend you a shirt. Also, a pair of pants if you want to wash your clothes. Hotels have facilities for that."

"But your clothes will be too big for me."

"Well, you can keep wearing the same clothes but you'll smell after a while. I may not be able to come close enough to kiss you."

I forced a smile. He was trying to be funny again, but I was still too agitated to appreciate it.

Lenny checked me into a hotel that night. The clerk stared suspiciously at us as I filled out the short guest form.

"How old are you? Do you have an ID?"

Lenny answered, "I can give you my ID. She's my sister and she's seventeen. She ran away from home so she's got nothing on her. I called my parents and they know she's here. They agreed to cool it off for a day or two. After that, I'll take her home or they'll come for her. I go to university but I'll visit her this evening, make sure she's okay."

The clerk regarded Lenny, for some seconds, without saying anything. Then, he held out his hand.

"Credit card."

Lenny handed him his card and the clerk flipped it over twice in his hand.

"You have different last names and you don't look alike."

"She's my half-sister. My mom married her dad. I kept my dad's name."

The clerk didn't answer. I doubted he believed Lenny's explanation, but he proceeded to take an impression of his card. He gave it back to him with the keys to the room.

In the room, Lenny dropped his body down on the bed and grinned mischievously.

"I can't believe how easy that was. I eliminated the need to smuggle myself in."

"How could you make up that story so quickly?"

"It's not totally made up. You did run away and your parents will probably come looking for you. And I'm truly a college boy, which inspires confidence."

That was the first night Lenny and I spent together.

The next day, he had classes and I saw him again early evening. He came with some Chinese take-out, his books, and some clothes, both for him and me.

"I didn't get a call from your parents or your aunt." He was frowning as he spoke.

"Good. Then, they don't care where I am."

I was relieved that I didn't have to return home. Not yet, anyway. But somewhere deep inside, I felt sad. Sad and disappointed that nobody seemed to care enough to find out where I was.

'Maybe, they believe you'll go home on your own. That must be it."

Lenny was still frowning. He seemed worried.

After we ate our take-out, Lenny needed to study. I went to take a shower and change into the shirt he brought for me. I also washed my underwear so they would be clean and fresh in the morning. Back in the room, I picked up the TV remote, but put it down again. I didn't want to disturb him.

There was nothing for me to do. I walked around the room for a little while. Lenny raised his head from his books and sat back on his chair to watch me.

"I should have brought you a book to read."

"It's okay, I've been reading all day at the public library. I came across it when I went out for some fast food."

Lenny had left me a few dollars for lunch before he went to school that morning. He nodded and went back to his books.

I went to bed. But I couldn't sleep, so I imagined playing the piano.

Hours later, he came to join me in bed. He touched my arm gently.

"Are you awake? I think we should think about what to do with you. You missed school today."

I burst into tears. I had not cried while I listened to my mother and my aunt argue, not when I confronted them, and not when I told Lenny about their argument.

I had cried when I ran down the hill. People saw me, but I had been overcome by anger and pity at myself and was hardly aware of them. This time, I exposed my unhappiness and my uncertainties in tears I poured out to Lenny. What was to become of me? No home really wanted me and I had no idea how to live by myself.

Lenny held me until I calmed down.

"I'll have to call Aunt Jola to tell her you're here. Maybe, she'll come get you."

I pulled myself away from his embrace and sat up. "Why her?"

"I know you feel more comfortable with her. And she's nice to you, isn't she? Besides, I don't know your parents and they sound a bit intimidating."

"Yes and Aunt Jola is nice to you, too." I glared at him. "How nice? Nicer than she is to me?"

"What do you mean? She's your aunt so how can
she be nicer to me?"

"You tell me. You've been with her at night."

Lenny bounced up from the bed and sat on a chair.
We stared at each other. My livid eyes dared him to tell
the truth.

"Did your aunt tell you that?"

"She told me enough."

"Then, why weren't you angry with me? You
should have been, as soon as you learned."

"I am now. I want you to make me understand
what happened."

He was thoughtful, avoiding my eyes.

"I went to your aunt's house around ten on
Wednesday after I had dropped you off several hours
earlier. I only meant to give her a check from my
parents, then leave. It's for Robbie's lessons and I had
forgotten about it. It had been in my wallet a few days.
I came across it as I was looking for something else. I
felt guilty that I forgot. On impulse, I decided to bring
it to her that night, in case I forgot it again."

"I know all that already, from Aunt Jola who said
you stayed twenty minutes. But a neighbor saw your
car there after midnight."

"I left a few minutes before midnight."

I was dumbfounded. Up to that point, I expected
him to deny that gossip. I turned away and covered my
face with my palms. I pressed my lips together to stop
my tears from coming again. I hurt terribly, but I
didn't want him to see me cry. I hurt when my aunt
betrayed me to my mother. This was much worse.

"Agnieszka, I don't want to lie to you."

He called me by my given name. He had rarely done so and I became more attentive to what he'd say next. But I also dreaded it.

"I didn't plan whatever happened that night. I saw right away your aunt was drunk when I got there. She had a bottle of expensive champagne on top of her piano. I thought it was odd she left it there because that piano is probably her most prized possession."

"After I told her why I came and gave her the check, she offered me some champagne. I refused it and said I had to drive back to the dorm. She insisted, and I thought if I took this one drink, I could get out sooner. So, I said, "a few drops." But she filled my glass halfway. When she handed me the glass, she sat down very close to me and started touching my chest."

"I ignored it because I knew she was drunk. I took a couple of sips, but she pushed the glass up my mouth and told me to drink up. I'd never seen your aunt like that, never imagined her in that state. She'd always struck me as so composed, so self-assured. There seemed such sadness, even desperation in her eyes. I took more sips."

"She started kissing me, groping me, unzipping my pants and I didn't have the heart to push her away."

"How could you?"

I cried, for the second time that evening. I was angry, bewildered, and distrustful of Lenny, my family, the whole world.

Lenny sat on the bed and tried to gather me in his arms. I shook him off and bounded from the bed.

"I don't ever wanna see you again."

"Please don't say that. I love you, Agnes. With all my heart. It's you I want to spend my life with. I haven't told you because you're still so young. But I thought, maybe, in two years, after I've graduated and got a job, we could get married."

"You're saying that to pacify me. How could you do it, Lenny? She's old enough to be your grandmother."

"I didn't do it for love or even lust. I had never seen such loneliness in anybody's eyes. She seemed to be pleading. She went on top of me and it wasn't at all like making love to you. If it'd been somebody else, I'm sure he'd do the same thing, unless he was hard and callous."

"I still don't understand it."

"I don't know that I can, either. It's not something I'm proud of. Even now, I cringe just thinking about it."

"She tricked you. She seduced you. But, why didn't you just get out right away?"

"I kept thinking about what happened that night. What I should or should not have done. I was only going to give her the check and leave right away, but she asked me to sit down while she poured the champagne. She took her time about it, too. She was talking and talking. She handed me the drink. Then, she was all over me on the sofa."

"I'm not gonna hear any more of this."

I covered my ears.

"I don't wanna be with you anymore, Lenny. Get out. I'll go home tomorrow morning."

"Aren't you afraid to be here all by yourself?"

"I am, but I'll survive. And someday, I'll pay you back for this hotel room."

"Can I come and pick you up at school on Friday afternoon?"

"No. I don't know. Don't."

He got up, dressed, and gathered his books. I went back to bed and pulled the bed sheet all over me.

I heard Lenny open the door. That was it, I thought. I'd never see him again. I waited, with bated breath, for the door to close.

"I love you, Agnieszka. No matter what happens, I think I'll always love you."

I almost kicked the sheet off me, and shouted, "Don't go. I love you, too."

But I couldn't.

*****

I left the hotel very early the following day and walked all the way home. My mother was already up, as usual, preparing breakfast. She looked surprised when she saw me and, wordlessly, let me in.

"Come have breakfast and get ready for school. You've already missed a day."

I followed her to the kitchen. The walk home took nearly an hour and I had worked up an appetite.

Minutes later, my father walked in, already dressed for work. He came up to me, and to my surprise, he kissed me on the forehead.

"I'm glad you're back."

Tata, like Mama, had always been uncomfortable with physical contact. I could remember only one time in my life when he held me close—when he used to let me sit on his lap while he read the newspaper. But, that ended when, at age seven, he told me I'd grown too big.

He and my mother took their usual places and we all ate in silence. I finished before they did.

"Thank you, Mama."

I'd been taught—and told—to say that after every meal ever since I could remember. I didn't always do so, but after I broke their rules by running away, I was anxious to please.

Mama said, "You're welcome. Come straight home from school."

I went straight home that afternoon. I'd never go back to Aunt Jola's. She was gone from my life forever. I'd been angry when she told on me to my mother, but Mama knew already that I had a boyfriend. That didn't matter now and seemed so far away, compared to what she did to Lenny.

I sat at the kitchen table for my cookie and milk. Mama sat down, too. She let me eat in silence.

"Did you stay with your boyfriend these past two days?"

I was dismayed. For me, the question came out of nowhere. I was worried that my parents would be very angry when I returned home after I ran away. I was afraid they wouldn't want me back. I couldn't believe it when Mama let me in without scolding me. I was grateful. Maybe, they missed me and were glad to have me home. I hoped they'd let the matter go, and we would all move on.

"I want the truth, Agnieszka. No lies."

"I didn't lie to you about Lenny. I just never told you about him," I said, without thinking.

Mama glared at me. She looked shocked. My answer shocked me, too. Two days away from home and breaking up with Lenny stirred something in me. Some independence, maybe? Defiance?

"I didn't ask who your boyfriend is. I asked if you stayed with him."

"Yes. I did. He put me up in a cheap hotel. I had nothing on me when I left."

"You're no longer a virgin, then." She sounded as grim as a judge delivering a death sentence.

"No, was I supposed to stay one?"

Mama got up in a huff, the legs on her chair scraping the already beat-up linoleum floor. She stood still in front of the sink, her back to me, her hands gripping its edges. I waited for her to say more, but for a few minutes, she was silent. I got up to leave.

"Don't go. We're not done yet."

She had been aware of my movements. I sat down again and realized, then, that I was trembling.

"You're graduating in three months and, in about five more, you'll be eighteen. I have taught you all I can. My duty to you is finished. You may leave any time after you graduate."

I couldn't answer. She blindsided me. I hadn't expected her to throw me out. Up until then, I worried that I'd always be in my mother's clutches. The past two days away from home, I felt her reaching out, pulling me back in, just as she had done less than a decade ago. I had hidden under my bed from her and her cod liver oil and she dragged me out by an ankle.

On the surface, she was cutting whatever bound us to each other. I would leave, yes, although I had no idea where to go. Cutting the strings didn't mean I was free or that she couldn't rein me back in.

"Is that all?" I tried hard to sound casual. I wanted her to think I didn't care, but she was still in control and she knew it. It was she who decided to chuck me from her life, making mush of my late efforts to lessen her power over me. I, alone, could break free, must break free. I understood that now.

"No. Clean up, after yourself."

She trudged out of the room without as much as a glance at me. That was new. In the old routine, after cookies and milk, I left her in the kitchen and went straight to my room to do homework until it was time for me to set the table for dinner.

The talk with my mother that afternoon was the toughest we've ever had and, for me, maybe the most important. I was restless in bed that night. But the fresh linens—warm and velvety—caressed my body, and the firm but supple pillows cradled my head and legs. I soaked up the pleasure they gave me. After cheap hotel accommodations during the last two nights, I realized I had taken these things for granted.

My mother shaped her world with too many restrictions, but she mastered many trappings of the good life. She chose the best linens. If she couldn't buy them, she sewed them herself. She was also a great cook, and the furniture she picked up at garage sales showed she had an eye for good design.

As I was falling asleep, raised voices from my parents' bedroom jolted me awake. I strained to listen. I guessed they were having one of their rare arguments. Next morning, after another wordless breakfast, I learned it was about me.

"Stay as long as you need to," Tata said.

I was walking away from the dining table and his voice came from behind me. I stopped and turned toward him. I had already made up my mind.

"Thank you, Tata. I really think I should leave. I'll have more than two months after graduation to look for a job and a place to stay."

I hid my anxiety. I had very little idea what job I'd qualify for or how to find it, or whether I could afford an apartment.

"I can keep my ears open for a sales job at the department store I work for."

"I would really like that."

I suspected I needed something better than a sales job to survive on my own, but for the time being, I'd be thankful for it.

That very evening, I fished out the paper Tata dumped in the trash. I perused job ads and listings for apartments and was appalled at how much it cost to rent. With no experience, I could get a minimum-wage job, but I doubted I could make enough to pay for the places I saw advertised. Being on my own was going to be tough.

Since that day, I no longer worried about my mother's opinion of how I spent my time. I still followed the morning and evening routines, but I also went out with friends at school whenever I felt like it. I often came home later from staying out, but I made sure to be home by dinnertime.

I couldn't explain, in those rebellious days, why dinner was sacred to me. Maybe, it was my affection for Tata. He loved me, and that was obvious when he welcomed me back with a kiss and went against Mama's decree to throw me out. Dinner was the one time we were together.

My mother, for the most part, let me alone from then on. Maybe, we both couldn't wait for those few more months when we would be free from each other. And yet, I did miss her after I left.

I thought, many years later, how sad it was that we often realized how much someone or something meant to us, when it was too late and we couldn't change things for the better anymore.

XII. Transitions

I missed Lenny. That spoiled rich kid had a sensitive, caring soul beneath his smart retorts, a side lacking among people I knew, both young and old. I did love him.

I missed him so much I was sure I would call him some time. But I decided to wait a few weeks, depending on how long I could bear not seeing him. Anyway, he should stew for a while.

But I didn't have to call him. On my second Friday back home, I spotted him on the walkway just outside the school, after my last class. He had probably been watching me before I noticed him. Even from afar, I could see he was remorseful. He had a lost little boy look about him. He was also leaner and had lost some weight. I hesitated a few seconds before I ambled toward him.

He didn't budge from where he stood. I fought an urge to run into his arms.

"Hello, Agnieszka," he said as I came abreast of him.

His voice quivered a little and he seemed indecisive. I hadn't seen that before.

"Hi, Lenny."

I glanced at him but kept my pace. His eyes were
so sad, pleading for forgiveness. I was touched, ready to
open up to him.

"I'll leave, if that's what you want."

He walked in step with me. I waited to answer
until we had broken free from the crowd rushing home
or meeting up with friends.

"Can I have an ice cream soda first?"

His eyes lit up and his mouth twitched into a shy
smile. "Yes, oh yes."

He placed his hand behind my back and led me to
his car.

"How about fish and chips, instead?"

I was about to protest. It wasn't four o'clock yet
and dinner at home was always on the table at seven.
The cookie and milk my mother used to have ready had
gone the way of our strained encounters. Down the
drain.

I peeked again at Lenny's face, so haggard and
gaunt that my first thought was he needed food. For
both body and soul.

"Okay, fish and chips."

I was aware we would have privacy at the fish and
chips drive-in. We wouldn't have a rowdy crowd to
help us hide our thoughts and feelings.

He ordered and we ate in silence for a few minutes.

"These are especially good today, don't you think?"

Those were the first words either of us uttered.
Lenny wolfed down the last spear of fish. I nibbled on a
French fry.

"Hotter, that's all. They taste the same to me."

"I must just be hungry, then."

"You lost a little weight."

"I didn't go out much to grab some food. Could you stand it if I order another for myself?"

"Yes, go ahead. You'll have to go to the counter."

He went to get his fish and also brought back a sundae.

"Want some?"

"No, thanks. You need it much more than I do."

Again in silence and with his ravenous appetite, he polished off his second order of fish and his chocolate and banana sundae in about ten minutes. I slowly finished my soda. He waited until I sipped the last noisy airy drops of cola.

"Have you forgiven me a little?"

I raised my gaze to his.

"Don't you think I've forgiven you a lot? If not, we won't be sitting here alone together. We'll be at the noisy soda fountain."

He smiled, but he still appeared hesitant.

"Do you still love me just a little?"

I took a while to answer. A few more agonizing minutes wouldn't harm him and I wanted to watch him squirm a little longer. He put me through many tearful nights for what he had done, and maybe I needed to see him suffer to wear out my anger. I forgave him, but I was still unsure I should have. Except, I did miss him and ached for him to hold me. Lenny was generous with what I needed most—his warmth and his tenderness.

"I think so."

He smiled, but he seemed shy as he peered into my eyes.

"Can I hold you?"

I looked away and nodded.

He gathered me in his arms and I laid my head on his shoulders.

"I'm so sorry I was so stupid. You don't know how much I've missed you, how miserable I've been," he whispered against my hair.

"I've missed you, too."

I was content to be back in Lenny's arms. Even as a child, I got so little warm human contact from my family. Not until I met him did I know the comfort and reassurance it gave.

"I told my mom about you."

I raised my head, dismayed. It was too soon for his family to know about me.

"No. Why? I was really hurt and angry, you know. I wasn't going to have anything more to do with you."

"That's what I told her. That you were so hurt and angry I would probably never see you again because of what I'd done."

"Did you tell her about Aunt Jola, too?"

"I had to. I was so devastated after our last conversation. I needed someone to talk to who'd understand. I told her everything I told you. Maybe, deep inside, I wanted her to punish me, but I also hoped she could give me some advice. I had to try to get you back. I didn't think I could endure not seeing you again."

"You can talk to your mother about things like that?"

"Yes. My mother's life revolves around her children and we have a special bond because I was an only child for six years. She's the reason ours is a talky, touchy-feely family."

"I envy you."

"You mean it, don't you, envying me?"

He was clearly touched, but how could anyone brought up like him really know what I'd been through?

"I think Tata is more accepting, but I can't talk to him like that. He'd be shocked. She, too, of course."

"I'm sorry, Agnieszka."

"I used to talk to Aunt Jola about stuff, but that's all over." I couldn't hide the sadness I felt for my family.

"I don't think I can face your aunt ever again. I go from my guilt, to anger at your aunt, and back to guilt. I can't figure out how she could have drawn me into her web."

"Her web—it is, isn't it? I was caught in it, too. What did your mother say?"

"She seemed in pain, too, like I was. You have to meet my mom. She has this enormous capacity to understand and actually feel what you feel and, somehow, that helps. She said something about opportunity. Your aunt was extremely lonely, needy for affection and a warm body and I was there. I was young, with raging hormones and she knew she could bend me to her will."

"Raging hormones. That's your excuse? You couldn't get out because of those hormones?"

"She didn't say that's all it was. It's also those other things that happened. The champagne, the pity, the late night. Please, Agnes, can you forgive me? I'll go to therapy, if that'll help convince you to forgive me."

"I've forgiven you. But I can't help getting mad at you and my aunt whenever I think about your tryst."

"It wasn't a tryst."

"Whatever it was, I can't just wish it away. Why didn't you run from there? Are those hormones really that powerful?"

"You're asking me that? You've seen them in action."

He glanced at me with a sheepish smile.

"They can't be choosy, those hormones?"

"That's not always possible, I'm afraid."

I pouted and shook his arms off me.

"Believe me, I learned my lesson. Next time, I'll run at the first sign someone is trying to seduce me. Unless you're the one doing it."

"I wouldn't know how to."

"Ah, but I don't agree with you there. I think, with you, it comes naturally."

"Is that something I'm supposed to be happy or proud about?"

"You should be proud and I'm happy to be your victim."

The Lenny I first met was back. The one never at a loss for words and could sweeten them when he needed to.

I settled back into his arms. How good it felt there.

"Did your parents ask who your boyfriend was?"

"They didn't ask, but they know. My mother remembers you from the time you drove her and me to pick up Aunt Jola at the hospital. She knows now it's the same car the neighbor saw."

"I see. Were your parents mad at you because of me?"

"At first, I didn't think they were. They didn't ask me about you, not even your name. But I was wrong. About Mama, anyway."

"So, she is mad at you?"

"Very. When I came home after running away, it was like nothing happened. But she was just holding back her anger."

I told Lenny how my parents treated me the morning I returned from the hotel. How I thought they were glad to see me back, forget what I did and move on.

"In the afternoon, I swallowed my cod liver oil, and Mama gave me my milk and cookie. It was back to the old routine."

"What's with the cod liver oil?"

"Long story. I've gotten used to it. She's probably right that it's good for you. Rich in vitamins and minerals. Anyway, she sat with me as I ate and asked if I stayed with my 'boyfriend' the last two days. I said "yes." She wanted the truth."

"So, the cat's out of the bag."

"Yeah, but she was mad. I wasn't her pure, virgin daughter anymore. She was done with me and told me to get out of the house by my eighteenth birthday."

"Your parents are troglodytes. Every girl I know at the university is no longer a virgin. Who ever heard of kicking a daughter out for that?"

"It's happened to me."

"I'm sorry. Obviously, they think sex is only for married people and maybe, only for procreation, but she was harsh—the way she told you to leave. Still, leaving home isn't a bad thing. At eighteen, you're an adult. Lots of young people are eager to strike out on their own. You may be better off. I left home before I was eighteen."

"You were going to college. You knew what you were doing."

"True, you might say my immediate future, at least, was laid out for me. I was off to college, and my parents have been paying for it. All I've had to worry about is getting good grades."

"I'm not like you. Except for my music, I don't know what I'm doing. Before I ran away, I don't think Mama meant to kick me out. They need me. I was born to take care of them in their old age."

"What do you mean?"

"All my life, I've picked up these messages from her that that's why they had me."

"Are you sure you're not reading too much into what she told you?"

"Maybe, but I've had this feeling since I was a kid. It's hard to shake off. I can't explain it any other way."

"Having a child for that reason is old-fashioned and it's too much to put on a young kid."

"I don't have to worry about it anymore, do I? They're kicking me out. I don't have to be afraid anymore that I'd grow old in that little room with one tiny window."

"It's a good thing, then."

"I feel better about it after talking to you. I'm free to live my life like I want. I can't believe it."

I was also frightened, but I couldn't admit that to Lenny, then.

"Does your dad give you the same vibes?"

"Tata's easy-going with me, but I wish he showed more interest. He didn't, until Mama decided to throw me out. I think they argued the night she asked me to leave. In the morning, he said I could stay, as long as I needed to. That's going against Mama's wishes."

"What are you going to do?"

"I'll leave as soon as I can before I'm eighteen. I don't have a choice. I'll get a job after graduation; maybe, an apartment as soon as I can. I'll probably end up rooming with someone. Other than that, I don't know. I'm excited to be on my own, but I'm also scared. I've always relied on my parents."

"I'll try to help. Maybe, we can room together."

*****

Peaceful, blissful weeks followed for Lenny and me. I now went out with him anytime I wanted to.

Mama no longer kept track of my whereabouts and acted indifferent to how I spent my time. Often, we didn't meet face-to-face until dinner.

The midnight incident between Lenny and my aunt continued to rankle me. Lenny and I never stopped talking about it, so often that he called it "the midnight seduction." Maybe, we needed to talk about it over and over until he could forgive himself and I could accept his explanation. Anyway, it began to sound ridiculous after we went over it so many times that I simply got tired of it.

A month later, Lenny asked if he could take me to meet his mother. But I wasn't ready.

I was still getting used to the idea of being on my own, free to make my own decisions, and do as I pleased. I needed to find out where it would take me and to build trust in myself. Only then, could I have the confidence to meet his parents. I told myself meeting them seemed so momentous and whatever happened, then, couldn't be undone. Or was I merely frightened about meeting his formidable mother?

At home, the strained relation with my mother withered into a habit. We both got used to it and, pretty soon, it didn't bother me anymore. I hoped it had stopped bothering her, as well.

I had other matters to concern me. Graduation was fast approaching. My teachers had long known my ability on the piano and they asked me to play a piece for the graduation ceremony, before the valedictory address. So I spent hours practicing piano between coming home from school and dinner. But more pressing, in my mind, was the life I had to create for myself after graduation. In the evening after homework, I perused ads for jobs and apartment rentals.

I was enjoying my busy but peaceful days, when they were jarred all over again the week before graduation.

Unlike my girlfriends, I didn't expect relatives or friends to see me graduate or perform at the ceremony. My parents would be there, and somewhere in the audience, so would Lenny. At dinner early that week, my father dredged up the matter of Aunt Jola's presence.

"I think you should invite your Aunt Jola. She taught you all you know about the piano and she should have the chance to watch you, be proud of you. She and Mama don't have to talk to each other, you know. I think the audience would be big enough, so we won't have to run into each other. Go invite her. Sending an invitation is not enough."

"I'm not going to her house and I'm not sending her an invitation."

I was being defiant and I avoided my father's eyes, afraid to see anger in them. He didn't raise his voice. He was annoyed, but was anxious to hear me out.

"Why not? She quarreled with your mother, not you. Over something that had to do with you, I might add."

Tata's even manner made me daring and I felt free to speak my mind. "I did not make them quarrel. They did that all on their own, but Aunt Jola betrayed my confidence and I can't forgive her for it."

"Whoa! Another piggy in the family. As stubborn as your mother. She already suspected you were going out with a boy, so how was it a betrayal by your aunt?"

"It was. You shouldn't tell someone else's secrets you promised to keep to yourself."

"Don't be childish. People will always do what they want, what's in their best interests. I think inviting your grandaunt might help get these two back together. Blood is important to your mother and there's only the three of you here to share it."

My gaze darted between Tata and Mama, and I wondered if she put him up to this. Mama needed Aunt Jola, but she had too much pride to initiate a reconciliation. In my mind, she was using me again for her own needs. Why could she not swallow her pride and woo her aunt back?

"Invite her yourselves because I won't."

I rose and headed for my room, the first time I left during dinner without being excused. I didn't rush. I waited for Mama's reproach for violating the sacredness of the dinner hour—the long, ritual of togetherness concluding our day. But it didn't come.

Although I hated to be in the middle of whatever was going on between Mama and Aunt Jola, that wasn't what held me back when I refused Tata's request to invite my aunt. I actually believed my mother and aunt were better off talking and confiding in each other, despite their jealousy or envy for what one had and the other didn't.

The truth was I was still angry and resentful about the "midnight seduction." I had long forgiven Lenny, but I couldn't forgive Aunt Jola. And childish or not, I still hurt deeply that she destroyed my trust in her by informing on me to my mother. I realized then how important a child's trust was and breaking it could lead to devastating consequences.

I suspected my parents didn't know about Aunt Jola and Lenny. Aunt Jola would never have told Mama she seduced Lenny. She would have been too ashamed. I also doubted that Mama disclosed her suspicions to Tata about a lover and the gossip about the midnight visit. She valued pride in family, second only to her belief in God. She might hate Aunt Jola, but she would protect her reputation.

I considered telling my parents about the "midnight seduction" and, maybe, they would see why I was defying their wishes. But, maybe, they really didn't care anymore.

From my childhood, my father didn't involve himself with telling me what to do. My mother and he had agreed that molding my behavior was her responsibility. I believed that was why he had always been easy on me, sometimes to the point of indifference.

I was more than mildly surprised my mother kept silent when I left in the middle of dinner, after I refused to invite Aunt Jola. In the past, she would have scolded me for being disrespectful and given me a lecture. It seemed she was determined not to have anything more to do with me.

Later that week, my mother reconciled with her aunt—probably on my father's prodding—and asked her to come to the ceremony. On graduation day, they sat next to each other in the area reserved for relatives. I saw them, as I took a slight bow on stage before I sat down at the piano.

I scanned the audience, searching for Lenny. He waved at me from the other side of the aisle, third down from those for relatives. Our gaze locked for an instant.

As I walked toward the piano, I saw Aunt Jola craning her neck in the direction where Lenny sat. Her nosiness bothered me and I scowled in annoyance as I stared at the piano keys. But playing always took me out of myself and as I focused on the keyboard so I could imagine the notes I was about to play, my concerns vanished.

The school asked me to choose a lighthearted piece lasting five minutes or less, preferably a popular, familiar one. I chose Debussy's *Clair de Lune,* a dreamlike and hopeful piece, but wistfully sad and uncertain. It evoked how I saw the future. It wasn't the happy, upbeat music my teachers wanted but I was sure many, among my class, saw what lay ahead the way I did.

After the last notes, I lifted my fingers off the keys and placed my hands on my lap. I sat for about a minute, just as my aunt did the first time she played for friends and relatives in her new house. The audience applauded. I stood, bowed, and smiled.

I played flawlessly and they liked my performance. Out of habit, I searched for Aunt Jola in the audience

and smiled at her. At that moment, I was ready to
forgive her.

XIII. Complications

When the ceremony ended, congratulating relatives and friends swamped excited graduates and I was trapped in a crowd of strangers. My parents weren't in the crowd, probably waiting for me to join them where they sat. That wasn't unusual. In past recitals, they used to stand back while Aunt Jola jostled her way to reach me. But even Aunt Jola didn't seek me out this time. She couldn't have dared. I was sure she believed Lenny had already related to me what really happened that Wednesday midnight.

My family could wait. I decided to find Lenny, but he found me first. He greeted me with a wide smile.

"You were magnificent. I love the piece you chose."

He held me and kissed me fully on the lips. I blushed with pride.

"You like dreamy pieces."

"Yes, like you. But you're number one dreamy."

"Did you see Aunt Jola?"

"She's here?"

Lenny scowled, his eyes quickly scanning the crowd.

"With my parents. They said such nasty things to each other, I thought they'd never talk again."

"Good for them. But I've got to go. I can't face your aunt."

"But you're not to blame. Raging hormones, remember?"

Lenny and I had reached a point when we chuckled at the mention of "raging hormones," as I did now. But not Lenny. He shrugged his shoulders, shuffled on his feet and forced a smile. I touched his arm in sympathy.

"I should go, too, anyway. My duty to my parents."

I felt letdown, although I knew that, with Aunt Jola there, Lenny wouldn't meet with my family.

"Can you meet me again on Friday? Maybe in front of your school? Same time."

"I can do that."

"Oh, here."

He fished a small box out of his pants pocket and handed it to me with a peck on the lips.

"Best wishes on the new adventure waiting for you in the big, bad, wide world."

He squeezed my hand and left. I clutched the box tight in my hand and watched him disappear into the dense rowdy crowd. I tucked the box safely into a zippered pocket in my bag.

My earlier impulse to forgive Aunt Jola faded with every slow step I took toward my family. I got sick to my stomach at the thought of meeting her again. I had tried to excuse her behavior so many times, convincing myself it wasn't so unusual for an older woman to seduce a young man and initiate him into lovemaking. People wrote about it so it was probably common enough.

But why hit on the man I loved? She was of my blood and ancient enough to be our grandmother.

Opportunity, Lenny's mother said. To me, that did not excuse Aunt Jola. Neither did her being drunk.

I felt like running away again. If Lenny had remained, I might have actually left with him. I stood where I was for several minutes, unable to take another step.

Where would I go, if I left now? How would I live? I could expect Lenny to help me for a few days, as he did that first time. Maybe, he could lend me some money while I looked for a job and a place to stay. But he might not have money to lend and I knew that, after a while, I'd feel guilty taking advantage of his kindness.

I sighed and dragged myself to face my family.

As I expected, my parents and Aunt Jola remained on their seats, oblivious to people milling around them. They didn't talk. They ignored each other, as if they were strangers who happened to choose adjacent chairs. I approached from behind and sat on the empty chair next to my father.

"Hi!"

"There you are. Congratulations, graduate." He shook my hand vigorously.

My mother smiled and handed me a large box tied with a wide red ribbon from past Christmases. She said nothing.

"Thank you, Mama."

I smiled sweetly back, always grateful to receive one of those boxes from her. I knew a beautiful dress she had sewn lay within, carefully folded and protected inside a clear plastic bag.

"Open it when you get home."

I wanted to shout, "Give me a hug, Mama. Tell me you're happy I've graduated and you're so proud of how I played that you could cry." Instead, I stared at the box in my hand and consoled myself with the anticipation of unwrapping her lovely creation in it.

Aunt Jola rose from her seat, sashayed in her high heels toward where I sat, and handed me a small box. She bent over to kiss me on both cheeks. I recoiled, but she grabbed me by the shoulders. I stiffened as she kissed me.

"You played beautifully. You're older, have seen more of life and it's given a depth to your playing. *Clair de Lune* is not exactly what I would have advised you to choose for this audience. A bit too ... too ... personal. *Hungarian Rhapsody*—that would be my choice. More impressive. A dramatic start, with several other dramatic passages after that. It's also familiar to many."

"I know, you told me. Passages from the last half have been used in cartoons. They gave me five minutes. *Hungarian Rhapsody* takes twice as long."

"Too bad. You could have displayed your skills much better with that piece. But I commend you for not choosing *Fur Elise*. It's beautiful, but too easy a choice and it's played too often."

"The music teacher suggested that."

"Aaayy." Aunt Jola rolled her eyes heavenward and laughed. With that gesture, we slipped back into the old, familiar ways we talked to each other, as if there wasn't a wedge between us. But I didn't forget that she broke my trust and I was still angry about it. She took the chair next to mine.

"Open your gift."

I hesitated.

"Maybe, I should wait until we get home."

Tata nudged me with his elbow. "Go ahead. Indulge your aunt. Open it."

"Let her wait until we're home, after we've had some refreshments. I made pierogi and a cake." Mama sounded irritated.

"Come on, what's the harm? I'm curious what could be in such a small box," Tata said, reaching over and pulling the ribbon off the box.

So, I tore off the wrapper and lifted the lid. Two exquisite blue stones, larger than corn kernels, glittered from the light that fell on them. Tata let out a low whistle.

I picked up one earring and twirled it on its post.

"My ears aren't pierced." I loved the gift, but I couldn't hide my disappointment that I couldn't wear the earrings.

"Not a problem. How about if I take you to someone who would do it? I'm surprised you haven't had it done," Aunt Jola said.

"Put it back in the box. Don't you know those are sapphires?" Mama snapped at me.

I glanced at Mama; her eyes were worried and angry. I quickly put the earring back in the box, placed its lid on and tucked it in the safest corner inside my bag.

"Someone will see what you have there and rob you. We should get out, now."

Tata said, "What's the hurry, Ania? It's crazy in the parking lot right now. I can't just drive away. We'll end up sitting in the car, waiting."

"We're making a spectacle of ourselves here. Better to sit in the car and wait."

Mama got up, pulling Tata by the arm. We all rose to follow her. I saw Aunt Jola shaking her head.

In the car, Mama said to Aunt Jola, "Did you have to ask her to open that gift, in view of the whole world?"

"I wanted to see her reaction."

"She knows nothing about precious stones."

I was annoyed that they were talking about me again as if I wasn't there. I butted in.

"No. But I do know sapphires are blue, and Aunt Jola won't give me fake stones. So if I had to guess, I'd say sapphires."

Aunt Jola smiled. Mama scowled and turned to Tata.

"Can't you start driving out of here?"

Tata scowled back at her but started the engine. "I'll get us out quick as I can, but promise, you all, to be quiet until we get home."

Less than an hour later, we were home, and had our pierogi, cake, and a bottle of wine Aunt Jola brought with her. The wine sparked off what followed.

Aunt Jola poured the wine and I accepted half a glass. I took my first sip, and discovered "heady." The wine tingled on my tongue, a little tart, a little sweet, a little bitter, and very pleasant. It sent a fruity essence up my nose, an essence as varied as its taste. It made me lightheaded.

I took more sips, one after another, a little too quickly. Within minutes, my glass was empty and my head swam. I raised my glass to my aunt, sitting across the table from me.

"Why do you drink so much, Aunt Jola?"

"What are you saying? I had half a glass, same as you. Your Tata already had two."

"Tata holds his alcohol better. You get really drunk."

"How do you know that? I don't think you've ever seen ...," Aunt Jola started to say, but she stopped and glared at me.

I glared back at her and she turned her face away. I was sure, then, that she knew that I knew about her and Lenny.

"Mama doesn't drink, maybe, because she's aware she gets easily drunk. Maybe, we three are alike. I'm already drunk."

I was provoking her to answer but she didn't take the bait.

"I had this much and my head's already light." I gestured with my thumb and forefinger to show the depth of the wine in my glass. I held my aunt's gaze. "So, that's all I'll allow myself. Is that so hard to do, Aunt Jola? Things happen when you drink too much."

Tata said, "That's enough, Agnieszka. Your aunt is an adult and can do what she wants, including get stinking drunk."

"Yes, she can. But she shouldn't go around seducing young men, like she did Lenny that night."

I wasn't thinking.

My parents stared at me in shock, frozen in place. A pall gripped the room. I endured some long minutes of dead silence.

Aunt Jola broke the unbearable tension. She clutched her purse and started to rise.

"I should go home." Her voice was a whisper and she avoided our eyes.

"Wait, Aunt Jola." Mama's commanding voice stopped her and she dropped back on her chair.

"Agnieszka, I take it Lenny is your boyfriend. He's the same young man who took us to the hospital to pick up your aunt the day she was discharged?"

I nodded, dismayed at the mess I started.

"That was his car parked at your aunt's house that midnight?"

I nodded again.

"I never thought to put those two together. I guess I don't understand these things. Is Agnieszka telling the truth, Aunt Jola?"

I stared at my mother and realized I had handed her a weapon she could use against her aunt and she was quick to grab it.

"The truth? I told Agnes the truth. She got a different version from her boyfriend. Who would you believe?"

She was hedging the truth and, to me, it was a challenge. After my outburst, I was determined to stay silent. But if truth had to come out, I wanted to be sure it was as accurate as possible. I had to say more.

"I believe Lenny. You told me he stayed twenty minutes. He admitted he left a few minutes before midnight. You were very drunk and very lonely. You forced him to drink and began caressing him. He took pity on you."

Mama glared at her aunt, a wicked glow in her eyes.

"Is that true, Aunt Jola?"

"What's it to you? Whatever the truth is, it's none of your business. Whatever happened, it was between two consenting adults."

"Consenting? But you seduced Lenny," I said.

"That was what he told you. Why didn't he run out? He let himself be seduced."

Lenny's "raging hormones" excuse popped up in my mind, but Mama spoke before I could.

"How could you do this to one who's more than a granddaughter to you, who took you as her model?"

Mama's accusation teemed with righteousness.

"I don't have to explain myself to you."

Aunt Jola rose from her chair, but my mother, reached over and held her arm.

"Then, why don't you give us your version? I'm trying to understand this. How could you seduce a young boy? You must be at least forty-five years older."

"What really shocks you? That I seduced him or that I'm so old? I'm human and I have human needs."

"Lenny told me she was very drunk and very lonely."

"That's no excuse," Mama said.

"Well, what's your precious boy's excuse? He had an erection and he made use of it," Aunt Jola said, glaring at me.

Mama gasped and I winced. Aunt Jola was losing the argument with my mother, so she struck at me. My anger rose again and I defended Lenny.

"Raging hormones and he pitied you. He went to give you a check that he had forgotten for his brother's lessons. You shoved the drink to his mouth and sat on his lap."

Aunt Jola grimaced with pain. She opened her mouth to speak, but Tata rose from his chair to cut her off.

"Enough! You're all making me blush. I'm ashamed of you all for bickering like this. Grow up, Agnieszka, things happen that hurt and make you suffer. You, Aunt Jola, act your age and get yourself a man nearer your age. And, get out of here now. It's best that you never come back."

Aunt Jola slung her handbag on her shoulders. She stopped behind my chair and spoke in a soft, trembling voice.

"I never meant to hurt you. You were right about being drunk. I'm sorry. And it's not Lenny's fault. Tell him I'm sorry."

She avoided my mother's gaze and left.

Shaking his head, Tata went to his armchair, muttering, "A messy business. Really messed-up."

He grabbed the evening paper on a side table and dropped his body on his armchair to escape within the newspaper pages.

Mama and I didn't move for some time. I wanted to run to my room and be alone but I was shaking so much I was afraid my legs would buckle under me.

"Are you still seeing that boy?"

"Lenny's sorry for what he did. I've forgiven him. I can forgive her, too, but I won't have anything more to do with her."

"Your Tata's right. This whole business is confusing. I know Aunt Jola has always been a passionate person. But still, she should have restrained herself."

I didn't answer. I had said the same things to myself. They helped, but not much; and after listening to Aunt Jola today, I felt sorry for her. Life was passing her by and her yearning lingered on.

I recalled snippets of conversation I heard as a child and suspected that Aunt Jola might never have known fully how it was to be made love to. She had married and, yes, it had been for love. Her husband, who I never met, apparently had great affection for her. But he couldn't love her the way she wanted him to.

Once, she had whispered to my mother the reason she never had children. I'd always been curious what it was until I learned how babies came into being. She had also remarked more than once about her vicarious thrill watching young people in love and I had caught her many times, gazing with a wistful smile at Lenny and me while we fooled around.

I felt sad for Aunt Jola—sensual, lusty, generous, and to me, at that moment, also tragic. All that was left for her was to long for, but never experience, the excitement, the pleasure of being made love to.

Nothing new surfaced that night, but I gained a better understanding of the "midnight seduction" and Aunt Jola. Myself, as well.

Mama and I resumed talking to each other after she broke with Aunt Jola, probably forever. Not that we grew chummier. We were never that way; but we had fewer uneasy silences and our ritual, washing dishes after dinner, became a quiet, pleasant way to be together. I hoped she finally began to see me as an adult.

She didn't express any wish to meet Lenny and wasn't any more curious about him than before. I suspected she distrusted him for his part in the "midnight seduction," but she never told me her misgivings about him. She might have decided not to interfere with what I chose to do.

I spent the week after graduation sleeping a lot. I was exhausted, both in body and mind, and I needed a short vacation to regain my energy and sense of balance. I was plunging into the new adventure of being an adult on my own, and it would require all that I had in me.

Sometime during that week, I asked my mother what I should do about the sapphires Aunt Jola gave me.

"Should I give them back? It doesn't seem right to keep them after what happened."

"She gave them to you. You didn't steal them. They're yours. Besides, you never know if they may come in handy when you find yourself in need of money. I have no idea how much precious stones sell for, but you can probably get a thousand or so for those."

I kept the stones. True, they could be useful, but they were more than that. They were a memento of those years of music, and learning to make music with Aunt Jola—years that were impossible without her; years that shaped me and would always remain a part of me.

Aside from the sapphires, I received a marvelous ruby heart from Lenny. Those precious stones were, to me, symbols initiating me into official adulthood. I wore the ruby everyday. I hung it from an old chain I used with other pendants. Mama cast a surreptitious glance at it many times, but never asked about it nor remarked on its beauty.

I rarely wore the sapphires although I had my ears pierced. I didn't tell Lenny about them. I had no desire to stir up bad memories.

As Tata promised, he found me a job in sales at the department store where he worked. I was grateful to have it, but I couldn't live on the wages I earned from it. It did give me experience in sales and dealing with customers. I discovered myself good at it and I decided that after a year, I would search for work in a music store. There, my knowledge and skills in music would come in handy.

I also began to think about leaving home.

XIV. Lenny and Me

"Did you mean it when you said we could rent an apartment together?" I asked Lenny on our way to a movie house one weekend.

"Why? Are you seriously considering it?"

"Leaving home, yes. Renting. I gotta get out by my birthday."

"I would rather room with you than with anybody else I could think of. Besides, I've been itching to leave that dorm. I think I'm too old to be bound by their rules."

"Yeah, I ask myself, why wait? I won't be any readier in a few months."

"I'm game if you are. My parents won't be thrilled, but they'll understand. You have a job. I have an allowance and I could ask my parents for a loan, if that's not enough. Between us, we can pay for a cheap apartment now. I'm graduating next year, so I'll get a job that pays enough for us to move to a better apartment later on."

"You make it sound so easy."

"With enough money, it is. Actually, this isn't the first time I've thought about this. When you ran away months ago and I wasn't sure what you intended to do, I hatched all this up in my mind. I know people— granted most are grad students—who live together in sin. It's more common than you think. A real sign of the times."

"I'm Catholic and have lived a sheltered life. Or have you forgotten? I'm sure my mother wanted me to remain a virgin until I got married."

"I do forget when we're in bed together. No inhibitions there."

Lenny grinned. I bowed my head in mock shame.

"I wanna be on my own and Mama's deadline is coming up in a few months."

"But you're not sure, about sharing an apartment with me."

"Scruples. Can't dump years of strict upbringing just like that."

"I understand, although I'd say you're doing very well."

"I have a job, but I can't afford an apartment on what I make. I don't know how long it'll take to find a roommate or how I'll get along with that person."

"Then, why not me? We get along swimmingly and I'm sure we can find a place in a week or so."

"You're a guy, that's why. But that's my parents saying that, not me."

"Do you really care what they'll say? They know about us and you'll soon be on your own, anyway."

"I care. But I doubt Mama ever really did. The things she's done for me, she was really doing for herself."

"So, what are you going to do? You have to leave and it may take you a while to find a roommate. I'm here and willing."

"You're right. I don't have much choice; so many things I still have to learn. I feel safe with you. Yeah, why not? Let's do it."

"What? Live with a guy without marriage? You're disowned, girl." Lenny gaped at me. He was being funny, again.

"But seriously, if I could get married right now, you're the one I'd ask."

"You've got no one else right now. Anyway, I'm not sure I'm ready for that. I'm a bit messed up—uneasy about leaving home and sharing an apartment with you, but at the same time, I can't wait to be on my own."

After dinner two evenings later, I told my parents I was moving in with Lenny. My mother sat, regarding me with eyes that could freeze the warmest heart. I was never able to read from her face what churned in her mind. But that evening, I didn't have to try.

Tata delivered me a blow worse than that look.

"We did tell you you're free and on your own once you graduate and I'll keep to that promise. But believe me, my impulse is to lock you up in your room until you're twenty-one. Living with a man you're not married to is bad enough, but to do it when you're not even eighteen yet—it's a disgrace. To you, to us, and to all that we believe in. We've tried our best to bring you up right. Where did we go wrong, Agnieszka?"

The muscles on my father's face twitched from pent-up anger. Anger that hit straight through to my chest. He had always been easygoing with me, so I thought he accepted my actions, though I was aware that, sometimes he merely resigned himself to my inability to live up to their expectations.

Tata didn't judge my actions the way Mama did. She controlled morals and behavior while he guaranteed food and shelter in exchange for comfort and the privilege to be left in peace. They were clear on their roles and stuck to them.

Mama said once that Tata had stronger ties to his religion and his Polish roots than she did. I'd never seen him go to church, pray before the Black Madonna, or touch a rosary, and I shrugged her remark off. I believed her now, as I sat across the table from them. I had deeply offended his morality and felt like someone on trial. I was near tears.

Minutes later, my mother's voice ended the painful silence. "I did say I wanted you out as soon as possible, your eighteenth birthday, at the latest. I'm glad you're doing something about it."

She rose from her chair and walked straight into their bedroom

I stole a glance at my father. If I still hoped he'd show me a little support, I was disappointed. He refused to look at me—his eyes cast down, his face masked by shadows, and his hands clasped tight on the dining table.

Back in my room, I set my alarm clock to wake me up earlier. I decided to take the bus to work the next day instead of riding with Tata. I'd enjoyed the pleasant car time alone with him, but he'd never been as angry with me as he was that evening. Maybe, he wouldn't want to have anything more to do with me. I must keep out of his way as much as possible until I could leave home for good.

The next morning, I dressed quickly, taking care to muffle the noise that could travel through the thin wall into my parents' bedroom. I tiptoed from the living area into the front porch, but as I was about to go down the stairs, I heard Tata whisper my name.

"Agnieszka! Wait for me. I'll just put my shirt and my pants on. We could grab breakfast at the drive-in down the hill."

He was back in his room, pulling the door behind him, before I could speak.

I nearly crumpled to the floor. From disbelief. From relief that he didn't throw me aside in his anger. I sat on the top steps and quietly let my tears flow. Tears I didn't allow myself the night before.

I dried my eyes when I heard my parents' bedroom door open and close again. I rose from the steps and waited.

My father came up to me, placed his arm around my shoulder, and led me down the steps. Neither of us uttered a word until we were in the car. He didn't start the engine and he sat quietly for a minute or so. I kept my gaze on my hands, clasped on my lap.

"I do love you, Agnieszka. I may not show it and I may object morally to you living in sin with a man, but you'll always be my child. I can't speak for your mother, but I'm sure she loves you, too. She has a harder time expressing it, and even I think she's too harsh on you."

I regarded my father with tears in my eyes, picked up his right hand, and kissed it. He placed his hand on my cheek.

"Good luck, my child. I wish I could do more, but I am what I am and I have to live with your mother. We've no one but each other now. We do love each other in our own way."

"I'll be there for you, too, if you ask me. Can't you trust me?"

"I do trust you. You've matured, though your mother may not think so. I trust you to choose wisely, live the life you want to live. I don't expect you to be there for me, as you put it. I've lived through a lot and I've survived. You must make your own way as I have made mine. It wasn't the life I dreamed of, but I'm at peace with it. You will be, too, with yours. Someday."

Two weeks later, I packed all my clothes into a suitcase—my first purchase with the little I earned at the department store. I took the dresses my mother sewed for me, even ones I had outgrown. They were meticulously crafted creations and they reminded me of the best about her. I put my few books, music sheets, and knick-knacks in two boxes.

Lenny came at precisely the time he promised. He rang the doorbell, which surprised me, but he did have a directness about him and abhorred secrets. My mother stayed locked up in her bedroom where she'd been since I started packing.

I opened the door to Lenny and put a finger to my lips to ask him to be quiet.

"Why? Your parents know you're coming to live with me."

"Keep your voice down. Mama could be asleep in her room."

I lied. Maybe, I was ashamed for him to see how gloomy my mother was and how she treated me.

"I was hoping to talk to your mother. I've only had glimpses of her. I bet, if you really look at her, she's as pretty as you are. Maybe, not as gracious."

He grinned, teasing me as usual. But I ignored his bantering.

"I haven't got much. Two boxes and a suitcase. Let's be quick about it. I can't wait to get out of this apartment."

Lenny followed me up the steps and into my bedroom. After we loaded my belongings in his car, I asked him to wait while I went through the room one last time for anything I might have missed.

I surveyed the room quickly. I had pulled the bed away from the wall, covered it with fresh sheets, dusted and polished the furniture to shining, and vacuumed the floor. I thought sadly—the room's no longer mine. If I left traces that I once lived there, they weren't visible to the naked eye. I turned off the lights and banged the door loud enough for my mother to take notice.

She didn't come out as I had hoped. So, I knocked on her bedroom door three times, waiting in between knocks for her to come out or at least say something. She did not. I wanted us to say goodbye to each other

and for her to wish me well. I walked out of the
apartment, with heavy steps and an even heavier heart.

Why my mother refused to see me off or wish me
well, I could only guess. I preferred to believe she
couldn't admit that she didn't want me to leave, and
she might have broken down to watch me go. But my
mother never cried, at least not in my presence.

Tata was at work when I left. He and I bid goodbye
in the car, when we got home from work the day
before. He actually had a tear or two pooling in his
eyes. We had to sit for several minutes to compose
ourselves before going up to the apartment.

Lenny and I took about five minutes to empty the
only place I ever lived in of everything I owned. We
moved to a cheap apartment within walking distance
from the university campus.

*****

The apartment Lenny and I rented had one room
nearly twice as large as the living/dining room at my
parents' place. It was spare, but clean, smelling of paint
and cleaning detergent. It was sunny from the large
south-facing window spanning its width. Our daily life
unfolded within the perimeter of the 300 square-foot
space.

It had meager furnishings—a double bed, a
loveseat that opened into a bed, an armchair, and a
square dining table with four chairs. Built-in shelves
flanked a large closet on the wall opposite the bed. A
narrow bar separated the small kitchen from the
living/sleeping area. Across from the kitchen was the

bathroom with a toilet, a sink, and a shower. It could only hold one person in comfort.

The building was close to the university and housed students in more than half the units. It had most amenities that appealed to them—a toaster and a microwave in addition to a cooktop and refrigerator in the kitchen area, coin-operated washers and dryers in the building basement, a modest gym, and a swimming pool.

By evening, on our first day in the apartment, we had finished putting away all our possessions and arranging the room to suit our needs. I had fewer things than Lenny, and they fit into less than half the closet. We filled the shelves with books, Lenny's stereo, and a small television he brought from his room at his parents' house.

We ended the day devouring take-out sandwiches, and watching television. We were exhausted and we went to bed early.

The next day, light coming through the large window flooded our bed, hitting my face and waking me up. I reached for my small alarm clock on the night table. Some minutes past six. I had a long wait to ten o'clock when I needed to be at work. At home, I usually didn't stir from bed until eight in the morning.

I glanced at Lenny, still soundly asleep next to me. Home was no longer on that hill. Home was now here where light arrived too early and irritating noise from cars and trucks forced life on me before I was ready to begin my day.

I got up to close the drapes and went back to bed. The drapes were not heavy enough to shut out light and even with my eyes closed, I sensed it all around me.

I lay awake, thinking about the life I had left, the new life with Lenny, and how unprepared I was to cope with the unknown challenges ahead. I recalled Tata's anger: "You're not even eighteen and living with a man you're not married to is a disgrace." He was right. I was young, ignorant, and scared. Most of all, scared.

What was I doing here? I should be preparing to go to college somewhere, preferably a music school. What was I doing with the talent I was supposed to have? I loved Lenny, but I wasn't ready for whatever future I was being sucked into. I wanted to make something more of myself, rise above the life my mother had.

On the surface, Mama seemed to have accepted her life, but she didn't have much joy or enthusiasm for it. I recalled everything Aunt Jola told me about her: finding herself in a strange country at such a young age, experiencing prejudice, and having to help support a mother and a sister who walked out on her. Was I facing a similar fate? Reduced to a life, surviving from day to day? For the first time, I understood and sympathized with Mama's frustrations.

I felt like crying, but I didn't want to wake Lenny. I got up, went to the bathroom, and closed the door. There, I sat on the covered toilet and let my tears flow freely.

Minutes later, I heard a soft knock on the door, but I was too overcome with sobbing to answer. Lenny opened the door slowly and came in. He stood before me, in the single space large enough for him around the toilet.

"Missing home, are you? Come." He bent over and kissed my forehead. Then, he pulled me up and enclosed me in his arms.

Was he right? Did I really miss home? Despite the narrow and often cold world it offered me, I had felt comfortable, cared for, and protected in it. I never had to think, much less worry, about good food, fresh sheets and clean clothes, or someone who would look after my health and care for me when I was sick. I did miss home, but my tears were, at least, as much for the uncertain future to come.

"I missed my home, too, that very first time I went to summer camp," Lenny said. I could almost hear the smile in his voice.

"You get used to it. I had so much fun during that first camp that I was eager to go the second time."

I said, "But this is more serious and I'm not a kid,"

"No. But, maybe, we can look at it like a camp. The first one you ever went to, away from the comfort of your home. Camp is a little slice of life, you know, organized around activities."

"I never went to summer camp or anything like it. I've no idea what goes on in it."

"This will be our own unique camp. You get to choose what we do in it."

He led me back to bed, made love to me, and I fell into deep asleep. Lenny was like that. In the few months we lived together, he was patient, funny, and loving.

My alarm clock woke us up at eight. We both got dressed although his classes started in the afternoon.

"I'll go out with you. We'll get some breakfast and I'll drop you off at your work. I'll go for groceries. We have nothing to eat in the apartment and I need coffee as soon as I get up in the morning. Do you know how to cook?"

"I can. That's one thing Mama insisted I learn. But she taught me elaborate Polish dishes—beet soup, mushroom soup, *bigos* which is beef stew with sauerkraut, stuffed cabbage leaves. Of course, I can do hamburgers and scrambled eggs, too, if you want."

"No, no. That all sounds yummy. I'm not picky about food and I'm sick of hamburgers and eggs, which were all we had at the dorm. But I won't eat pork."

When I came home that afternoon, the small refrigerator was stocked with packages of beef chunks, kielbasa, red beets, cabbage, onions, and potatoes. There were also eggs, two gallon-bottles of milk, a big jar of sauerkraut, butter, and bread.

I decided to make *bigos*. When he tasted his first forkful of it, Lenny said, "This is really good. Now, I'm sure I won't marry anyone else but you."

About a month after Lenny and I moved in together, I met his parents. His mother had explicitly asked him to bring me to dinner.

I was apprehensive. My parents all but disowned me when I moved in with Lenny and I suspected his parents also struggled to accept our living together. I wondered if they were going to look me over. If they didn't like me, would they persuade him to leave me? But from all his stories, his mother impressed me as warm and caring, and his parents as open-minded enough not to care that I was Catholic.

By the time we went to dinner at his parents' home, I had talked myself into believing I was eager to meet his family.

My eagerness was justified. Lenny's parents were open, spontaneous people who welcomed me with hugs and kisses on both cheeks. I must have looked bewildered as I returned their embraces because Lenny gave me an amused smile.

After dinner, his mother asked Lenny's brother, Robbie, and me to play for them. I hadn't touched a piano since leaving home and the chance to play again was enough to inspire me to perform my best.

When I finished, Lenny's mom gave me more hugs and kisses. Her eyes were moist.

"What a precious gift you have, Agnieszka. Nurture it. Come more often and practice here."

On our way back to the apartment, I babbled on about what an unexpectedly nice evening I had, and how touched I was by his mother's reaction to my playing.

"Mom's mom was a big-hearted, very expressive Italian who married a Sephardic Jew. Everyone who saw her said she looked like Anna Magnani, a famous Italian actress long ago. Her spirit lives on in us."

"Robbie, too?"

"Him, too, although you wouldn't know it because you only saw him at piano practice. He's awfully serious about that. But he's played a few practical jokes on me. Dad is the laid-back one in our family. You see his smile more in his eyes than his mouth."

XV. Parting

Hopes nourished me in those months; hopes I sometimes realized in words, if not in action. I took Lenny's advice, bought a little notebook and wrote little plans for the immediate future in it. How wonderful if they had all come true without a hitch. And yet, how unrealistic.

I was happy living with Lenny. Blissful, in fact. For about three months.

He came home late from school one night. He'd never done so before. He said he'd been neglecting his studies since he and I moved in together and he had to catch up. With the semester nearing its end and finals to study for, he didn't have much time to spend with me.

I was disappointed, but I understood. The rest of that week, he came home late. I assumed he was studying in the library. On Friday night, he told me he had to visit his parents—alone—that weekend. I sensed tension in his voice, but I didn't ask him about it.

That weekend was the first time I was alone in the apartment. On Saturday morning, I spruced it up and in the afternoon, I went to the library, took home an armful of books and magazines, and read until dark. I spent the evening glued to the television, nibbling on chips out of a big bag on the coffee table and sipping soda from a can. That was dinner.

For me, this was something new. At home, dinner was like a ritual—done at the dining table at a specific time; begun with a short prayer; followed by soup, starch, meat, and vegetables; and finished with desert. Except for the prayer, I tried to preserve the practice as much as I could with Lenny, but more often than not, we ate take-out or leftovers straight from cartons.

It occurred to me that, when we were together, Lenny and I would be so absorbed in each other that we hardly noticed what went on around us. The television could be blaring and we wouldn't be able to say what was playing.

I had trouble sleeping that night. I had begun to sense that Lenny was slowly building a wall between us. I wondered if he had met someone else at the university, a student more beautiful and smarter. How could I, an unworldly girl fresh out of high school, compete with someone like that?

The thought troubled me but I dismissed it. I couldn't believe he could fall in and out of love so quickly. I convinced myself he was telling the truth, that he was swamped with all he had to do to close the semester. That was all there was to it.

But what was the visit to his parents all about? Did he need to talk to his mother again about something that concerned me? Or, was there some crisis or problem that recently surfaced in his family? That would easily explain why he was so tense and why he had retreated into a shell. Maybe, he would tell me when he came back.

I spent Sunday making pierogi, half with cabbage and ground beef and the other half with stewed dried apricots. Lenny had never had pierogi and I wanted to show him how much I missed him by making something special. They took time to make, but I knew his taste in food by then, so I was sure he would love them.

He came home much later than I anticipated, when I was already in bed. I had put the pierogi back in the refrigerator.

He climbed quietly into bed, as if he was afraid to disturb me. I stayed still, my eyes shut tight. He lay on his side and went to sleep. The following morning, he was up early, had coffee, and left after giving me a quick kiss on the forehead. He said he had to go to the library to study.

I was left on the bed, confused and flooded with a premonition that everything was about to end between us. As soon as he closed the door, I burst out crying.

I was late to work that day. I told the floor manager I woke up with cramps and nearly called in sick. I had a good work record and she believed me.

Lenny came home as late as he had done the past week. I was determined to find out what was going on and I asked him that evening.

"Can we put this off until finals are over? I'll be done in two weeks."

I wanted to be reasonable so I nodded, but I had to look away to hide my disappointment.

We fell back into some of our old routine in the days that followed. We had breakfast together, got dressed, and he dropped me off at work. He still came home late, but I waited to have dinner with him. But dinner didn't change from what it had been the last few weeks. He ignored me, opened a book, and studied while we ate.

We only talked about the day's trivial goings-on. Who he saw at the library. The customers who came into the store I worked for.

On the second Friday after I asked to talk to him, he surprised me. He came into the store a few minutes before I finished work and took me to an old haunt, the soda fountain. We hadn't been to it for months.

"Finals over?" I had to shout over the din around me.

"Two more, but they're easy subjects for me. Expect me home earlier."

I felt relieved. Maybe, things were getting better and we no longer needed that talk we were going to have. That night, he made love to me. But I sensed some reserve new to him.

The following week after finals, he came to pick me up at work, as he did the Friday before.

"Are we going for an ice cream soda?"

"No, we're going for fish and chips but we'll take them home." Lenny's voice was low and he didn't smile.

In the past, he grinned and licked his lips, anticipating hot, crunchy fish and chips and the sauces they came with. I felt that premonition flooding me again.

We ate in silence, broken once in a while by my remarks about the food, to which he nodded or mumbled "Yeah, good." Neither he nor I made a move to clear the table when we finished eating—a chore we used to do without thinking, in our impatience to cuddle on the sofa and share our little anecdotes for the day. For a few minutes, we sat without saying a word. Lenny continued to avoid my eyes.

I was tense, unsure what would happen, racking my brain for what to do next. But I was also filled with dread that kept me silent. I gripped my hands tight on my lap and waited.

When Lenny finally spoke, his voice was soft and steady.

"I can't do this anymore."

Those weren't exactly the words I imagined he would say. I had expected him to explain, to be contrite and miserable before he dropped the bomb on me. With those words, our ending seemed so abrupt and so final that 'stunned' was not enough to describe what they did to me.

My mind went blank. I got up and, before I knew what I was doing, I swung my left arm with all the force in my body and my palm landed on his right cheek. He teetered on his chair, but he managed to set it back squarely on the floor.

I ran to the bathroom and locked the door. I sat on the covered toilet seat and stared blankly at the wall. No tears came, but I was angry and confused about a reality I couldn't accept. I believed Lenny had betrayed me. The second person I loved to do so.

How could he go from loving me so passionately to coldly casting me aside? And how was I to survive without him? When I could no longer focus on my music, he came along and filled that void in me, but I had nothing now to fill that emptiness.

Another void. An abyss, this time. With no one and nothing to stop my descent into it.

Many minutes later, I heard footsteps. I hoped they would stop outside the bathroom door but they kept going. My heart sank. When I heard the front door open and close, I knew it was really over.

I bawled my eyes out then. How was it possible that something so beautiful and promising could end with those words, simple but like a loaded gun? *I can't do this anymore.* More than once, he said he wanted to spend his life with me. I believed him. He sounded so sincere. And yet, he was gone and all was over.

I got out of the bathroom, my face still drenched with tears. I sat by the dining table. Lenny had cleared it of the dirty boxes and plastic utensils from our meal. Our favorite meal together. Our last meal together. On the table was an envelope with my name written in his large hand.

I picked up the letter with trembling hands. He hadn't sealed the envelope. In it were two pages he had probably written earlier.

The letter had no date on it and was simply addressed "Agnieszka."

I know you won't believe me if I say nothing has ever pained me more than writing this letter to you. But that's the truth. I never meant for it to end this

*way. I have loved you more than I have ever loved
anyone before. Believe that at least if you doubt
everything else.*

*I am weak and I am scared. This last year has
taken more out of me than I am capable of giving. I'm
also selfish. I would like to get back to what I was
before we met. But I know that would be impossible.*

And: No, there is no one else.

*The rent on the apartment is paid, for the next six
months. Please don't think this is an attempt to
appease the anger you justifiably feel toward me.
You've been paying more of the rent than I have the
last three months and I'm merely attempting to even
things out. I'll admit it eases my conscience a little,
although I know you will forever think me a prick and a
jerk.*

*I wish you luck and, someday, I hope you will
forgive me. I don't know why but I can't find it in me to
wish you love. That's how selfish I am, you see. I want
to keep that love all to myself even when I know I can't
return it.*

Lenny

I put the letter aside, too shocked to grasp fully
what it meant. It didn't appease my anger nor did it
make me understand Lenny's actions any better.

I spent the weekend in bed, in disbelief and utter
confusion. I went to work the following weeks, mostly
to keep my mind off my misery. I had lost interest in
life as I had known it. Nights were extremely tough.

One day, I came home from work to find Lenny's books, clothes and toiletries gone. He had left his stereo and his television. His keys were on the kitchen counter. This time, there was no note, no explanation. I burst out crying again and wished I had kept one of his shirts, the one he last wore and still smelled like him.

*****

A month after Lenny left, I missed a period. It didn't bother me much because it wasn't entirely unknown to me. But I began to really worry when I missed a period again the following month. I bought a pregnancy test kit. The result came out positive. To be sure, I went to a free family planning clinic and got the same results. They also told me to expect a baby in seven months.

There I was, eighteen and pregnant with a child whose father had abandoned me. I was still reeling from the pain he caused me—pain that seemed like it would never ease up. And, now, it seemed I was being tested again. I felt as if all the burden that could be bundled up in the world had been dumped on me.

I couldn't make up my mind whether to tell him or not. I was still angry and hurt, and I convinced myself I wanted nothing more to do with him. Ever. But what about the child that was to be born? I could hardly pay for my rent; how was I to care for a child on my wages? And in four months, I needed to vacate the apartment. As cheap as it was, it ate up my whole paycheck.

Abortion was, for me, unthinkable. Although I no longer followed the rituals of my religion, the principles I learned about the preciousness of life were deeply ingrained in me. In any case, the window for legal abortions was fast closing in on me.

I had to do more than the minimum I'd been doing to exist, for my child's sake. I had to contact Lenny, but he didn't make it easy for me to do so. He left no phone number and I never asked for his parents' address. I took it for granted he would always drive us there. I remembered that I did have his parents' phone number. Somewhere.

I took out Lenny's last letter. Maybe it would give me some answers to help me cope with all I've been dealt these past weeks. I read it again. Slower this time, pausing once in a while to let what I just read sink in.

I didn't know what I expected. The first time I read the letter, I was too dazed to understand it. When I finished, I was more confused than before. Somewhere in the letter, he seemed to be telling me he still loved me. If he still did, why did he leave? The reasons he gave me didn't satisfy, but it did convince me that he meant our parting to be final.

I needed someone to whom I could unburden myself, pour out my unhappiness. I had no one else but my parents—two people who would judge me harshly for this latest disappointment I was foisting on them. But, I was in despair, willing to settle for someone who would listen. Tata might.

That weekend, I visited my parents in late afternoon. I hadn't seen my mother since I moved out, but I had occasional lunches with my father when our schedules at the store permitted. I used to pass by the alteration department every morning and wave at him. When Lenny left, I shrunk into a shell and saw no one including my father.

My parents were surprised to see me, as I expected. Mama opened the door and stared at me for a while. I tried to smile. Although she didn't know yet that I was pregnant, it seemed she was already judging me. Or, maybe, she had this power to induce guilt in me. She didn't smile back, but she acknowledged my presence with a slight lift of her brow. Then, without a word, she opened the door wide to let me in. I entered, in silence.

Tata was sitting in his armchair, as usual. He put his paper down on his lap and smiled. He seemed happy to see me.

"I haven't seen you in a while. I asked your manager if you were sick and he told me you'd been coming in to work."

"I'm sorry, Tata. I haven't had much energy for the last few weeks and I've been dragging myself to work."

"Are you pregnant?"

My mother's question struck me like an arrow hitting a bull's-eye. Lenny's last words angered me enough to swing at him; hers stopped my breath and froze me where I stood. I realized, then, where her power over me came from. She had this ability to see through me so clearly that I could never hide anything from her. And she was merciless in letting me know what she saw, and in judging me for it.

Tata was speechless, his mouth open in disbelief, his worried eyes waiting for my answer.

I had no choice but to admit the truth. I nodded my head. I didn't trust myself to speak. One word could break my fragile hold on my emotions.

My mother smiled grimly. Was she triumphant that she guessed at the truth, or that she broke me down, or that *I* told the truth? It didn't matter. I had tossed power and control back to her.

"I would not have you parade your pregnancy before the neighbors or the customers I sew for. You're a disappointment to us, Agnieszka. I should have known. You take after your Aunt Kryztyna—you look like her, behave like her, and are just as ungrateful. I helped her go to college. But what did she repay me? She defied my mother's admonition, ignored my pleas, and ran off with her boyfriend. She was lucky he married her."

She peered closely into my face and shook her head.

"But you're not so lucky are you? Did that rich Jewish boy up and leave you when he found out you were pregnant?"

"He doesn't know I'm pregnant."

"Tell him. He should take responsibility. You can hardly support yourself on your pay, how do you expect to support a child?"

She was right, from a practical standpoint, but I was too emotionally bruised to agree it was what I needed to do. I was not ready for the pain that was sure to come from talking to Lenny.

My father hadn't said a word since Mama's devastating question. I watched him as he sat, scowling, refusing to look at me, his hands clutching the paper on his lap. I wanted to run to him, to kneel at his feet and ask him to forgive me for not living up to his trust. He raised his head, as if he sensed that I'd been watching him.

"How could you let this happen to you, Agnieszka?"

"I don't know, Tata. We took care not to get pregnant. Sometimes I think I'm the most unfortunate girl on earth."

I ran to my old room, overwhelmed again by misery and self-pity. There, I burst out crying. I had been crying, off and on for weeks since Lenny left. I didn't think I had any more tears left. But that evening, they flowed once more until, in sheer exhaustion from past nights of fitful slumber, I fell asleep.

The room was bathed in soft light coming through the tiny window when I awoke, startled by a knock on the door. I had slept through the night, something I was unable to do since Lenny left. I forced open my eyes, crusted from tears that had dried up on my lids and my lashes.

I knew it had to be Tata at the door. Mama never knocked. She barged in. I got up and dragged myself toward the door.

Tata knocked again before I could reach it. "Agnieszka, it's eight o'clock. Aren't you going to work?"

I opened the door. I couldn't look up at my father's face. I wasn't ready to deal with the reproach I might see on it.

"You slept in your street clothes," he said.

"I don't have anything here to change into. I didn't mean to fall asleep. I meant to go back to my apartment last night."

"Since you're dressed, can you leave now? We'll get breakfast at the drive-in down the hill."

I nodded. In the living room, I snatched my bag off a side table and followed Tata to the stairs.

He took us to the drive-in, where a line of cars had already formed. I didn't have any appetite, so I asked only for coffee. He gave the server my order and asked for a large empty coffee cup. Then he ordered a carton of milk with his coffee.

In the empty cup, he mixed my coffee and all the milk.

"You should eat well. You're eating for two."

He handed me the cup with a smile. "Are you sure you don't want an egg and ham breakfast sandwich?"

"I can't. I'm afraid I'd throw up at work."

I dutifully sipped the milky coffee, as I regarded my father in awe. In one simple solicitous gesture with the milky coffee, he told me, wordlessly, that he accepted me despite my having disappointed him.

The warmth of the coffee soothed my insides and I finished it in a few short minutes. I looked up at my father, who was still sipping his coffee, looking straight at the cars passing by on the street in front of us.

"Do you forgive me for the shame I caused you and Mama?"

He placed his cup on the dashboard and turned to me.

"I told you once that whatever happens, you're still my child. You're facing a trial, a hard one for you because you're so young and inexperienced. But we're all tested. Many times. Life's like that. It's what you do to deal with what's thrown at you that'll make you strong. I'll help you the best way I know how. So, don't hesitate to come to me for help. I won't promise not to get angry or blame you, but I'll do what I can."

I sat, still and silent, my eyes cast down, biting my lips to hold back tears of relief. When I felt a little more in control of myself, I took my father's hand, kissed it, and looked up at him in gratitude.

He wiped a tear from the corner of my eye with his thumb and smiled at me, his eyes full of sympathy.

We sat facing each other for a while. Neither of us spoke anymore until my father started the car and headed for work.

My father's precious, hopeful words kept me sane and focused for weeks to come. His inherent compassion, more than the challenge my mother's perceptiveness induced in me, gave me the courage to do what I needed to, not for myself, but for my child who was yet to be born.

XVI. Moving On

I found Lenny's parents' phone number in the drawer of the nightstand next to the bed. I didn't call right away. I needed to work up courage and rehearse what I should say.

Lenny's mother answered. She treated me with as much affection as she had in the past.

"Hello, Agnieszka, my dear. How are you doing? I've missed you."

"Good evening, Mrs. Weisz. How have you been?"

"Fine, I'm fine. But how about you?"

"Mrs. Weisz, I have to talk to Lenny. He tells you everything. So you know we've broken up. I really didn't want to bother him. But there's something he should know."

"I see. Listen, my child. Can it wait until we can talk face-to-face? I have something I wanted to tell you, too. Would you object to meeting me for coffee?"

"No, that would be nice. I think of you as a friend. It doesn't matter that Lenny and I ... " I couldn't continue.

"Good. I'd like you always to consider me as your friend. Would tomorrow be okay, after work? In fact, why don't we have an early dinner together? I'll pick you up right in front of your store."

Mrs. Weisz, was waiting in her car outside the store entrance when I got out of work. From there, she drove toward her home.

"I have this craving for barbecued ribs and I know the place to get the best."

"You eat pork? Lenny wouldn't touch it."

"They do have beef ribs. That's what I usually order."

"Are they as good?"

"Not as luscious. You know my mother was Italian and my father grew up in Spain where they adore roast suckling pig. Mother and I sometimes snuck out by ourselves and had the pork ribs."

The restaurant she took me to was open but empty. Spicy sweet smells from the kitchen flooded the dining room.

"My kids love this place. It usually doesn't fill up until after six so we'll have the place to ourselves and we can talk undisturbed."

I picked up the menu, but before I could go through the long list of barbecued meats, Mrs. Weisz spoke.

"Would you mind so much if I ordered for us? I promise to get something you'll like."

After the waiter took our order and left, Mrs. Weisz fished something out of her purse. She handed me a card.

"First things first. Let me give you this from someone we do business with. He runs a music store although he mostly deals in pianos. We get everything

Robbie needs there. Anyway, he needs someone who knows music and can play the piano."

I took a moment to read the card.

"Call him soon. He pays well, better I'm sure than what Gimbel's pays you. I recommended you to him. The job is as good as yours."

"Did Lenny put you up to this?"

"Oh, no, no. They had someone on that job two weeks ago, but he left and the manager asked if I knew someone. I thought of you right away."

"Thank you. I can really use this right now. I'll call him first thing tomorrow."

"Good," Mrs. Weisz said with a little smile.

Her smile faded as she regarded me closely. She stared at me for so long that I felt self-conscious.

"How are you holding up, my child? I've never seen Lenny so miserable and I'm sure you must be, too."

"Then, why did he leave me?"

Without thinking, I blurted out the question I had been asking myself these past weeks. The next moment, her words came back to me and I was astounded: Lenny was miserable. I had not expected that, or his mother's genuine concern.

"He didn't tell you the reason, did he?"

"He told me he was tired of me."

"Is that what he said?"

"Not in so many words. But that's how I read his letter."

"He wrote you a letter?"

I nodded. "He also said our love demanded more than he's able to give."

Mrs. Weisz shook her head, her eyes dark with sadness. I was baffled. Did she so understand how Lenny's leaving affected me that she could feel my misery?

The waiter returned and placed our order on the table. The hot, generously sauced ribs released a strong essence of garlic that made me nauseous. I grimaced and turned away.

"What's the matter, my child? Is it the garlic? They do put a lot. We can order something else for you, if you wish."

"No, it's all right. These look scrumptious. The feeling will pass. It often does. I'll start with the French fries."

"Eat, then," she said, doubtfully.

I nibbled on the fries before I took my first bite of one rib. It was delicious.

"Is this beef?"

Mrs. Weisz's eyes glinted with amusement and mischief, the way Lenny's did.

"No. You'll be my partner in crime from now on."

The offensive garlic smells did diminish and I was able to eat two of the three ribs on my plate. Mrs. Weisz finished hers off. She wiped her hands on her napkin.

"You said you had something important to tell Lenny. Would you tell me what it's about? I can tell him for you."

"Can I tell him myself?"

That profound sadness I saw in her eyes returned.

"I'm afraid you can't. He won't see you."

It took me a moment to take those words in.

"But how do you know?"

"That day you called, I talked to him and he told me so."

My tenuous control cracked. If I needed more convincing that Lenny had cast me aside, Mrs. Weisz just offered it.

"But he has to. I'm pregnant."

"*Madre de Dios!* That explains the garlic."

She rose from her chair, sat next to me, and gathered me in her arms.

"Just when you think things are bad enough, they get worse."

"I didn't expect this. He used rubbers."

"I know, I know. Things happen. But we'll have to do something. How far along are you?"

"Almost three months. I'm keeping the baby."

"Of course, if that's your choice. But there may be complications."

Mrs. Weisz gazed at me for what felt like minutes. I was learning the expressions on her face. She had the tendency to stare intently into a person's eyes. But she wasn't seeing me. She was deep in thought.

"You're right. You should talk to Lenny, and he should explain himself instead of hiding behind a letter. He should hear about your baby directly from you."

"Come visit us on Saturday. Stay the weekend and we'll sort through all this. I'll have Lenny pick you up before noon. He will refuse but I'll insist on it."

I smiled, grateful to her, but anxious about seeing Lenny.

She added in a tone that was sad and serious again,
"Let me warn you, though. I don't want you to be
disappointed. I doubt very much that Lenny will return
to you. But he should take responsibility for your child,
if you decide to keep it."

*****

I wondered, knowing how stubborn Lenny could
be, if his mother could really make him come to pick
me up. At half-past eleven on Saturday, I heard a
knock on my door. I opened it with an anticipation I
couldn't suppress.

Yes, there he was, standing at my doorway, leaner
in a striped shirt open low enough to show a little dark
fuzz on his chest. A stray lock of hair, hovering over his
right eye, emphasized his schoolboy charms. Despite
my anxiety, my heart fluttered with excitement. For an
instant, I thought I saw love and longing in his eyes,
but he blinked and scowled, and it was gone.

"Hello, Agnieszka. May I come in?"

"Yes, yes. Come in please," I answered in
confusion.

"May I sit down?"

"What?"

"May I sit down?"

"Yes, yes. Sit down please."

He sat on the chair and I, on the loveseat opposite
him.

"My mom said you had something very important
to tell me."

He fidgeted in his chair, his gaze darting everywhere. But he refused to look at me.

"I think it's best you tell me here. I may lose my courage to hear it in a house teeming with my family."

Revealing my pregnancy to his mother had been easy. She had been kind and supportive. But Lenny was nervous and he acted as if someone had put a gun to his head. He sat on the edge of the chair, hunched over his knees, his head bowed, his arms folded on his chest.

"Why don't you look at me? Have I become really repulsive to you? What happened to us, Lenny? How could you change so quickly? What did I do to kill your love for me?"

I wasn't going to dig up the immediate past. But if my presence was a threat to him, I had to understand why. Tears I couldn't hold back flowed down my cheeks and I bowed my head.

When I got a better grip on my emotions, I wiped my face dry with my hands and raised my head. Lenny sat in the same position, except his hands were now clasped in front of him and his head was lower, as if he was hiding his face. I watched him for a few minutes. He didn't stir from that position. Not once.

I realized then—he wasn't going to say anything— and it spurred me into action. My unhappiness, my self-pity turned into anger. I wanted him out of my sight, away from me that instant. I found the courage, or maybe the push I needed, to tell him about the baby. But not before I told him what I thought of him.

"You're a coward, Lenny. And you say you're selfish. So, what I'll tell you won't matter to you at all.

That won't be a surprise. But you should know. I'm
going to have a baby. Our baby."

He jerked his head up and stared at me. His eyes
were moist and red and his face was puffy. I was
surprised to realize he had been crying.

"That can't be. I was very careful."

"I'm sorry, but it's true."

I was amazed at how calm and in control I was
after my tearful outburst.

"How lucky can I get? Fallen again into that 10%
failure rate." He spewed out those words bitterly and
bowed his head again.

I didn't grasp what he was saying. He kept his
head down. I was still puzzling over his words when he
raised his head again and spoke without looking at me.

"You can't keep the baby. How far along are you?"

How could he ask me that, without so much as a
glance? I ignored his question.

"Keeping the baby is not your decision. It's mine.
It's my body."

"But the baby is equally mine."

"It doesn't have to be. You're free to forget us.
Many men do that. Get a girl pregnant and, then, leave.
I'll be okay."

He looked straight into my eyes, and I saw so much
pain in his that I regretted what I said. A look of love
and longing flashed across his face again. I fought an
urge to go to him, to tell him: *Hold me, Lenny.*

He regarded me a long time, saying nothing. His
mother was right. He was miserable. Worse than that,
he seemed hopeless. Desperate. I was confused. Was

our break-up as painful to him as it was to me? I wanted to take back my bitter words, but I was afraid my control would crumble.

At last, he spoke.

"I'd like to tell you now that I'm deeply, deeply sorry. I haven't said that to you yet. I wish things had been different, but some things are ... totally out of our control, like who we're born to and what we're born with."

I heard his words but, except for his regrets, their meaning was lost on me. He paused and averted his eyes, hesitant to continue.

"What are you saying, Lenny?"

"My mother believes I should tell you everything. But, I don't know if I can. Maybe, reality is too much for me right now; maybe, in a few years, I can accept it and talk about it. But I won't be here."

"What reality, Lenny?"

"I can't say it."

"But why? What about me? I hurt so much. I'll grasp at anything you tell me. I've got to know why."

Again, I caught that spark on his face, but this time, it seemed mixed with desperation. He was hurting at least as much as I was and, maybe, so much more.

I didn't think then. I took a few quick steps and kneeled on the floor beside him. I embraced him tight. His body started to convulse and he put his head on my shoulder and cried.

When he had recovered somewhat from the rush of tears, he raised his head.

"All I can get myself to say to you is, for the baby's sake, he shouldn't be born."

"It's too late for that. I want this child, Lenny. I want to keep a part of you."

"But he doesn't have a future."

"What do you mean? Tell me, please."

"I don't have a future. And there's a fifty-fifty chance that he or she won't, either."

"Is something wrong with you?"

"Yes."

He peered into my eyes with an intensity that reminded me of his mother.

"I could live fifteen to twenty years, more likely less, but they're probably going to be very difficult years, and I don't know how long it would take before I turn into a vegetable. Much sooner than those fifteen years, for sure."

Shock. Fear. Despair. I couldn't tell which emotion was strongest. All I knew was an icy wave went through me all the way to my toes and I had to struggle not to faint. Those words he uttered amounted to a curse, a curse he couldn't escape, an end to all his dreams, including a future we might have had together.

"You're young, Agnieszka, and so alive. You should take the most life can offer you and you can't do that with me."

I gazed at him, at the face I loved so much. I finally understood why he left. He had done so for me. I opened my mouth to speak, to tell him I would bear his burden with him just so we could be together. But he put his fingers to my lips.

"Don't. I can't live with the guilt. Make me happy by living. Write to me. Tell me how you're doing. But don't ever come to see me. That would only hurt us both."

By now, quiet tears were streaming down my cheeks. I studied his face, to remember its every detail, its every expression at that moment. I might never gaze at it again.

"You'll have a child to take care of. You seem determined to keep him. But be prepared that he might not be with you for as long as you want."

He wiped my cheeks with the back of his hand. Then, he kissed me all over.

"I have never stopped loving you, Agnieszka. And I won't, to my last breath. But the best thing you can do to love me back is to live life to the fullest. I'd hate to see it wasted away taking care of me. And I'd hate for you to see me become a slobbering shell, who you'll have to clean up. I want you to remember me as I am now."

"Hold me, Lenny. While you're here with me now. We've got such a short time."

I choked down my tears.

"Oh, Agnieszka, you don't know how I looked forward to it. The years we could have had ...."

He pulled me up off my knees, onto his lap and gathered me close. We clung to each other for a long time.

"I have some inheritance due to me. I'm sure my parents would agree if I ask them to pass it on to our child. On that, at least, I can be sure. You and our child will be provided for."

"I don't know what to say."

"Nothing. It's the least I can do. Raising him or her is a responsibility I should be sharing with you. I should be with you through your pregnancy, when our baby's born, and as he grows up, but I don't know how long I ...."

I clasped him close. "Stay with me this weekend, Lenny. At least leave me these last good memories of you. I need them to erase the past few weeks."

He nodded his head and I felt his tears on my cheek. "I need them, too."

"What are we going to do about your mother? She expected me to stay with your family this weekend."

"They'll understand if I don't return this evening."

*****

Despite our despair over Lenny's fate, those two days were some of the happiest I had ever had. We forgot the future on those wonderful days. We saw no one else but each other. The crowd at the soda fountain didn't exist for us when we went there again. We relived all the happy times we had together, relishing every moment, storing them up for the future.

We lingered in bed on our last day together, his arms around me.

"I was thinking last night about how you feel being an unwed mother, what with your Catholic upbringing. Maybe, we should get married."

"Then, you'll stay with me?"

Eyes mournful with regret, he gazed at me, caressing my face.

"I can't. I can't have you suffer anymore, and it's easier on me if we end things on the good memories we have."

"So, it's a marriage in name only. You mean to make me respectable, is that it? This is the seventies, Lenny. We have sexual freedom and women's liberation. I won't be the first unwed mother."

"But, maybe, it'll mend your relationship with your parents."

"My relationship with my father doesn't need mending. We hardly talk, but it's because he's respecting my mother's wishes to leave me on my own. As to her, yes, she'd probably be thankful. In her mind, it's the respectable thing to do. But I don't think it will change anything between us. You're doing much more than I ever imagined. Many men just disappear."

I was determined not to cry when Lenny finally took his leave. Happy memories were good memories and I wanted my smiles to be the last glimpse he would have of me. Plastering them on was easy enough.

But I couldn't control the sadness that roiled in me below the surface and I hoped that my eyes didn't reveal it too much. Sadness, I learned at that moment, was different from misery. I accepted the sadness, but I rebelled against the misery. Misery was, for me, treacherous, with a lurking desire to exact revenge on whoever caused it. Sadness was charitable, forgiving.

We clasped and we kissed, reluctant to let each other go, but aware every second that we couldn't put

off parting for much longer. Lenny pulled away, and
after one last long look at me, he strode briskly toward
the door, closing it behind him until he disappeared
from my sight. I heard him running down the steps.

I sat on the bed, staring blankly into space for
some time.

Lenny left traces of himself in the apartment and I
gathered them up and put them in a box. The comb he
borrowed from me, the toothbrush we picked up at a
small corner grocery store, the towel he dried himself
with after a shower. Of his voice and his face, his touch
and his warmth, his kisses and caresses, memories were
all I had.

A week later I got a call from Mrs. Weisz. She told
me she opened an account at a bank in my name, as
specified in the terms of a trust their lawyer was
setting up for my still unborn child. Funds would be
deposited into the account every month and she
suggested I move to a better apartment. In fact, she
would help me look for one. She also said she would
visit me often.

I was incredulous. I had planned to stay at the
apartment beyond the months Lenny had paid. I saved
money from not having to pay rent in those months. I
had worried about what to do after that, but the job at
the music store came up. I could continue to pay rent, if
I was careful with my money.

Then, this unexpected legacy came within a week
of my parting with Lenny. I didn't stop to wonder if I
should accept it. My child needed all the chance he
could get, which the legacy would help ensure.

Mrs. Weisz was true to her word. Within a week, she helped me find a new place, and I was calling her by her first name: Elise. (*Yes, my daughter, you were named after her.*)

I ended up renting a one-bedroom apartment in the same building. For me, it was luxurious. Its main room was nearly as large as the one I was vacating and the bedroom had a queen-size bed and enough space to accommodate a crib. I didn't have to wait to move to the new apartment. The building manager applied my unused rent on the previous one to my new place.

The following month held much more hope for me. I started the new job at the music store and Elise Weisz came to meet me once a week. She also called me every morning on the last weeks of my pregnancy, to ask how I was doing. She was the mother I always wished I had. The mother I wanted to be.

She told me what was going on with Lenny and I sent him letters through her. I learned Lenny returned to the dorm, but was always home on weekends. He was determined to get his degree even after he was diagnosed with his illness, the name of which I knew by then.

I planned to learn more about the illness, but not yet. I figured I had enough time. I would first enjoy this being growing inside me, who had been kicking and tumbling and forcing me to take notice. He was gradually becoming the whole world to me.

One day, Elise told me Lenny was graduating.

"Can I go to his graduation? I'll make sure he doesn't see me. I'd like to watch him walk up that ramp to receive his diploma. Then, I'll leave."

"We ourselves aren't going. In fact, he isn't going."

"But why?"

"He says it's all ceremony, empty symbolism. What matters is that he's done the work and he knows it. He's still as pigheaded and as smart-alecky as ever."

I chuckled and there were tears in my eyes.

"He intends to be productive for as long as he can. He'll spend his days painting and designing furniture. He says he'll even try composing music. This is one time I thank my lucky stars we're rich."

I asked, "Lenny's illness—it's inherited, isn't it? Who from?"

"His dad."

"He's still alive and you had a life together. So, why couldn't Lenny and I ...?"

"My husband was diagnosed in his mid-thirties after both Lenny and Robbie were born. That's where the difference lies. The prognosis is grim for early onset."

She paused, took a long breath, and let it out slowly.

"My husband, very likely, won't live through his fifties which are going by too fast. His symptoms are already pretty pronounced. That's why you saw him very briefly when you came to visit. He's ashamed of his disabilities."

I saw, then, the deep sadness in her eyes. Sadness I knew so much about. I was struck by the courage it took for her to keep her life sunny and hopeful and for her to set aside her misfortunes to care for those she loved, including me.

I hugged her to my heart. Tight. She wet my cheek with her tears, the way Lenny had done weeks ago.

When she regained her composure, she pulled away and held my shoulders, at arms' length.

"You are, to me, the daughter I never had. Be happy, for my sake, for Lenny's. You're capable of so much love. Go out there and build yourself a new life."

XVII. A New Life

I loved my new job at the music store. The owner/manager, Mr. Lazar, was a gentle man in his fifties who loved music but never learned to play. He mumbled something about being tone deaf. On my very first day, he shook my hand vigorously and spent more than an hour showing me his merchandise and giving me tips on how to handle customers.

He knew I was pregnant. Elise Weisz apparently told him even before I started work at his store. He said he would give me leave to have my baby if I made an effort to return as soon as I could. He was kind, but cautious.

The music store was quiet and not as busy as the department store, where people streamed in and out constantly, and many came merely to browse. There, some came to buy, but very few talked to me and asked about the items they were thinking of buying. Quite often, all I had to do was hover around, and if a customer decided to buy, I wrapped their purchase, and rang it up in the cash register. The work was mind numbing, but it helped me survive.

At the music store, the few people who came in were frequently interested in pianos and they asked questions. Mr. Lazar instructed me to play the piano for people who expressed even the slightest interest so they could hear how the piano sounded. I usually played the opening bars for potential buyers, but once in a while, someone asked for the whole movement or piece.

Mr. Lazar also encouraged me to play when no customers were in the store. He said it often attracted someone to come in. Once inside the store, he might not buy an instrument, but he could pick up some music sheets or other things he might remember he needed or wanted.

One quiet afternoon, on my second month at the store, Mr. Lazar approached me after I finished playing a sonata.

"You play exceptionally well, Agnes, and that's good for my business. I'm lucky to have you."

"Thank you, Mr. Lazar. I love to play and I can do it here all day. Getting paid is a bonus."

I glowed at his gratitude. He laughed.

"Well, I'm glad I can help you indulge a habit. Actually, I should thank you. I sold a couple more pianos last month. I think the customers liked how you played and were persuaded to buy here, and not at another store."

"Oh!"

I was gratified I helped his sales, but I was wonderfully surprised that my music could persuade a customer to buy.

"Listen, how would you like to go to a concert? It's the least I could do to show my appreciation."

"I've only been to one, months ago and I loved it."

"I have two tickets for a string quartet at the university music hall this coming Saturday. You could have them. I get tickets from various customer organizations, but my wife and I can't always use them."

"I'd love to have them. But one is all I really need."

"Well, they're yours. I know no one else to give them to. You may find someone to go with."

He went into his office and, when he came out, he handed me the tickets. The concert was for the coming weekend and since it was at the university, I could easily walk to it.

On the afternoon of the concert, I began to worry that I accepted Mr. Lazar's tickets too eagerly. I had never gone anywhere on my own except to school, work, and the supermarket. The concert was in the evening and, although I knew where the music hall was, I had never been to it. I decided to go that afternoon to see how long it would take me to walk to it.

I got to the hall in fifteen minutes. I stood just outside the lobby, where announcements for the evening's performance were posted on the walls. The lobby was still closed, and I peered through the glass doors and walked around the hall. I thought that if I was more familiar with the place, I wouldn't be so anxious.

I began to prepare for the concert two hours before it started. I chose a dress I often wore to work, and put on a little lipstick. I wanted to look nice, but not call attention to myself.

I arrived at the music hall half an hour before the concert. The only people around were me, a couple waiting outside the lobby, and several people standing in line to buy tickets. Ten minutes later, more people came and ushers opened the doors to the lobby.

An usher told me where to go as I passed through the door. Another usher at the door to the orchestra section showed me to the row where I had my reserved seat. I looked around me. The auditorium was small, compared to Heinz Hall, and probably sat less than 1000 people. I was alone in the hall for several minutes before others started to come in.

I enjoyed the concert very much. I'd been afraid of going by myself, but it didn't bother me as much as I had expected, maybe because I had looked around the hall earlier.

The following Monday, I told Mr. Lazar how much I enjoyed the concert. Since then, whenever he got tickets for performances at the university, he offered them to me. The events were not all musical offerings. Some were dance or theater, and I attended them all.

I relied on those performances for my entertainment. Along with Mrs. Weisz's visits, they helped vary my days, working and going through the mundane demands of living.

My social life was limited to what Elise Weisz called our tête-a-tête. Every week, she and I met, often at a coffee shop and, sometimes, at the restaurant where we had pork ribs. Our conversation always started with me asking about how Lenny was doing.

I was thankful for those uneventful first three months, working at the music store. By then, I was five months pregnant. I had gained a few pounds, but in a loose shirt and pants two sizes more than I usually wore, my growing belly was barely showing. One day, that month, Elise brought along a camera and took a picture of me. I faced her but stood sideways, holding my tummy. It was Lenny's idea. He wanted to see how I looked pregnant.

I was adjusting better, by then. I had accepted that all I would have of Lenny were memories, treasured ones kept alive by the child growing inside me. I had started playing a little game with myself shortly after he and I parted for good, a game I never shared with anyone, including his mother. The Vietnam War had ended a few years before, and I pretended he had gone to it and was missing in action—a small, private lie that helped me cope. "Missing in Action" meant to me he was alive, but somewhere I never heard of.

Around that time, I went to a concert by a chamber music quartet performing with a pianist. They were playing two pieces by Schubert, a well-known, well-loved piano quintet and a lesser-appreciated piano trio. The trio was what I couldn't wait to listen to. I had heard it before, as background music for a movie Lenny and I loved.

I arrived ten minutes early. I was quite familiar with the hall by then and I went directly to my seat in the orchestra, in the tenth row. A young couple who were probably students at the university, had already settled themselves next to my reserved seat, which was to the left of the man.

I sat down and made myself comfortable on the narrow chair. I couldn't help eavesdropping on the conversation of the couple to my right. The woman was explaining to her date what to expect in the concert. She spoke with so much authority about music and the performers that I was sure she was a musician studying at the university. I felt a pang of envy.

Just before the lights were dimmed before the performance, I looked behind me and up at the balcony. On this Wednesday night, the place was only two-thirds full. The group was playing the same program the coming weekend.

The pianist, the cellist, and the violinist opened with the piano trio. As I had expected, it was exquisite. The second movement stirred such sadness in me that, when it ended, I had to wipe away the moisture in my eyes. To my surprise, I found my cheeks were also wet. I'd cried without having been aware of it.

I felt embarrassed and as I raised my hand to wipe my face with my fingers, I glanced at the young man sitting to my right. He was watching me from the corners of his eyes. He wore an amused smirk that irritated me. I dried my cheeks and craned my neck in his direction. This time, I stared defiantly at him.

He stared back, his eyes frank and unembarrassed, amusement gone from them. I saw curiosity and concern in his large piercing blue eyes. He had brown hair slicked back into a ponytail, hanging a few inches below his shoulders. He had annoyed me, but I couldn't help wondering who he was.

Two weeks later, a young couple, vaguely familiar, came into the music store. The man, quite tall and lean, walked behind the woman, who came straight toward me. She struck a commanding presence—tall, probably three or four inches shorter than him; shining reddish brown abundant hair flowing down her back; a shapely figure clad in a shirt clinging to her torso, paired with bell-bottom blue jeans hugging her thighs.

"Do you carry music by Franz Schubert? I'm looking for his E-flat piano trio," she said in a voice I had heard before.

I must have frowned in my attempt to place her voice.

She added before I could answer, "Do you have any idea what I'm talking about?"

I couldn't help smiling. That same superior tone belonged to the woman lecturing the man at the last concert I attended.

To confirm my suspicion, I peeked at the man behind her. He was indeed the one I sat next to at the concert. He was examining something on his shoes, his head down, his shoulders hunched, and his hands in his pockets. I sensed his discomfort.

"Yes, I do. The first piece they played at the music auditorium at the university two weeks ago."

"Oh, you know it. Great. I'd like a copy."

She smiled; a smile full of teeth and crowned with crinkled eyes.

"I'm sorry. We had three copies, but we sold them all the week after the concert. We have more on order. They should arrive Monday, next week."

"Oh, how annoying. Can you reserve a copy for us? We'll come back next week."

"Sure. What name should I reserve it under?"

"Put my name down. Lydia Morgan. Mr. Lazar knows me."

She hesitated for a moment.

"On second thought, why don't you also put Charles Halverson, in case I can't come to pick it up. You okay with that, Charlie?"

"Fine."

Charlie's voice was deep and pleasant.

I expected them to leave at that point, but Lydia lingered as if she needed something more.

"Is there anything more I can help you with?"

"A classmate tells me someone here plays the piano extremely well. I know it's not Mr. Lazar. I've known him for years. Is there anybody else who works here besides you?"

"Not that I know of."

"Then, it must be you."

"I play, but maybe not as good as music students at the university."

"We'll see. Would you mind playing something for us?"

"Well ...."

In fact, I was reluctant. She was arrogant and that irritated me. I reminded myself that Mr. Lazar would expect me to comply with a customer's request, but he wasn't there and had taken that afternoon off. I could refuse.

She must have sensed my hesitation. She stared directly into my eyes, challenging me.

"Playing for customers is part of your job isn't it? There was a boy here once who did that. He was very good, but he had some ways to go yet."

Maybe, that remark decided it for me.

"I'll play, but I'll have to stop when customers come in."

"Okay. Do a short piece. Do you know *Liebestraum* #3?"

I was not about to be dictated to by her.

"Yes, but I haven't played it for a while. I'll do *Hungarian Rhapsody*."

It was a piece customers often asked me to play, so I had much practice doing it. For some reason, although I thought her irritating, I wanted to impress this woman.

I stayed seated for about a minute after I finished playing. My audience of two was quiet. I got up, with a hasty peek at their faces. I knew I had played well.

"If there's nothing more I can help you with, I'll go do something else. Please feel free to browse around."

"You are good. You don't sound like an amateur at all. Who's your piano teacher?"

Did I detect admiration in her voice?

"Thanks for the compliment. You don't know my teacher. She's my aunt. She played in concerts when she was very young."

"Really? What's her name? I might know her."

"No. That was in Poland."

"Oh! Anyway, you should study at the university, hone your talent, make connections with people who can help your career."

"I wish I could, but I earn just enough to support myself."

"That's too bad. Ah, well. Thanks for playing."

She jerked her head toward the door.

"Charlie, shall we go?"

I glanced at "Charlie" who was staring at me so intently that I had to avert my eyes. She tugged at his arm and they left. At the door, he looked back at me.

*****

The following day, when Mr. Lazar was back at the store, I asked him who the person was I replaced.

"Robbie had this job before you."

"Robbie? Mrs. Weisz's younger son?"

"Yes. He seemed to have been enjoying the job, but he only stayed six months."

"Did he tell you why he left?"

"Something about applying to the university. But he's not going until next year and I had encouraged him to play anytime we had no customers to attend to. So, if practice was what he needed, he could do it here."

"I heard competition is really tough. I think he wants to be sure he gets in."

Mr. Lazar's disclosure made me curious and when I met Elise Weisz that week, I asked her about it. She didn't tell me anything new or different from Mr. Lazar's information. I couldn't help wondering if

Robbie had quit, or been asked to quit, so I could have the job. If so, I owed so much to Lenny's family and to the child I was carrying. If not for them, I'd be eking out a living on my department store wages, and I'd be back at my parents' house or rooming with a stranger.

On Tuesday, Mr. Halverson came to pick up the music sheet I reserved for him and his girlfriend.

"Lydia couldn't come today so I offered to pick it up."

I nodded as I opened the drawer where I stored the sheet, already packaged in an envelope.

As I was ringing the purchase up, he said, "You play beautifully and you're beautiful."

I felt a blush spread all over me. Except for Lenny, I had been immune to the admiring male gaze, both during our time together and after we parted. But I felt uneasy about this man's gaze, probably because it was too much like Lenny's, especially during our early encounters.

I handed him the envelope and the receipt for the purchase.

"Anything else you need, Mr. Halverson?"

I pretended to count the money in the cash register, and kept my eyes focused on the bills.

"I'd like to hear you play this piece."

"It needs a violin and a cello, in addition to the piano. You don't get the full impact without all three."

"I see. So, without those two, this piece won't induce you to tears?"

I raised my head, anger welling up from within me. My voice was low, but I failed at my attempt to control my anger.

"It's none of your business when I cry."

"I'm sorry. I didn't mean to be intrusive. My friends think I'm a little too polite so I don't know why I even brought that up."

Still angry, I didn't answer. My reaction surprised me. Anger at an innocent bystander who had earlier witnessed my tears was too much. I was brought up to hide strong feelings, particularly those that showed how vulnerable I could be. But sometimes I failed, as I did that concert night and as I was doing now. I was terribly annoyed that I couldn't control my emotion.

"I'm really a nice person." He waited for me to speak.

Within my line of sight, I saw Mr. Lazar hovering around. I had to respond.

"I don't know you, Mr. Halverson. The way I was raised, crying is a very private thing strangers shouldn't see."

"Actually, I thought it very touching. I've never seen anybody brought to tears by music, not even Lydia who gets so absorbed in music she can forget you're there."

"We're all different."

I hoped my tone sounded as neutral as I meant it to be.

"Yes, so it seems. Well, thank you so much for your time," he said sympathetically, and left.

That night, I mulled over my encounter with Mr. Halverson and realized anger was my way of protecting myself. His interest was too obvious, and I wanted to repel it.

I never expected to see him and Miss Morgan again, but on Friday, he came into the store in late morning with two covered paper cups in his hands.

"I come with a peace offering. I hope you and your boss drink coffee. If not, I may have to drink both cups and I'm laced with caffeine already. I also brought chocolate chip cookies. I figured those are safe. Everybody seems to like them."

He placed the coffee on the counter by the cash register and took out a small white paper bag from a leather satchel slung by a strap across his chest.

I had to smile.

"I do drink coffee, and I know Mr. Lazar is a caffeine addict. He has a coffee maker in his office. It keeps going all day. And I'm like everybody. I love these cookies."

I took a cup of coffee and a cookie from the bag and approached Mr. Lazar. Mr. Halverson followed.

"This gentleman here brought us coffee and cookies, Mr. Lazar."

"Oh, how nice!"

He smiled at Mr. Halverson, who handed him his coffee and cookie.

"Here you are, Mr. Lazar. My way of thanking you for your wonderful service."

"You're welcome and thank you. But I don't know you, young man. I saw you here for the first time a few days ago, to pick up an order. Are you going to be a regular customer?"

Mr. Halverson chuckled. He seemed eager to be nice to Mr. Lazar.

"In truth, I know little about music and I prefer folk rock. My curiosity about classical music is quite recent. I was drawn into it by a friend who's a music student. She's been teaching me a little about it."

"Oh." Disappointment crossed Mr. Lazar's face for an instant, but he recovered quickly and he grinned broadly at Mr. Halverson.

"But who knows? A budding interest in classical music may lead you back here. You do have a name?"

"Charles Halverson. Miss ...?"—he turned to me, raising his eyebrows—"knows my name."

"Let me introduce us both. I am Felix Lazar and my assistant is Agnieszka Talar. But she will answer to Agnes."

The two men shook hands. I stood beyond the reach of Mr. Halverson's long arms, so he bowed to me with a smile.

"If you're not a music student—and I can tell you go to the university—what do you study, Charles?"

Charles smiled. He had beautiful teeth, white and perfectly formed.

"Thank you for not calling me Charlie. People seem to do that without thinking. I don't like being called Charlie. But to answer your question, I am going for a Ph.D. in economics."

"A Ph.D.! And in a difficult field. I'm quite impressed."

Mr. Lazar shook his hand again, more vigorously than before.

I was also impressed, but it was the remark about his name that brought a smile to my lips. It reminded me of a similar one Lenny had made when we first met, except in his case, he preferred the more informal Lenny to Leonard.

"So, Charles, where do you think our economy's heading?"

Mr. Lazar grasped Charles' arm and led him into his office. Charles threw an apologetic glance in my direction. I drifted toward the cash register, sat on a stool, and slowly finished my coffee and cookie.

It was nearly noon when Charles left.

XVIII. A Future

Charles came two or three times a week bringing coffee and cookies. He never bought anything, and during the short quarter hour he stayed, he talked to Mr. Lazar. On the third week, he barely glanced at me as he handed me a cup of coffee.

"Can I talk to you before I leave?"

He seemed as embarrassed as he did the day he came in with Lydia Morgan.

"Okay. I'll walk you out the door when Mr. Lazar lets you go."

I grinned, unable to hide my amusement. He grinned back, one eyebrow slightly arched. "He does love to talk, about the 'state of the nation,' he calls it. It seems there aren't too many people he knows who care enough to talk about it. I have to remind him every time that I have a class to go to."

Charles must have found some excuse to cut short the usual conversation he had with Mr. Lazar. After a brief exchange, he walked toward the piano bench where I sat and played *Clair de Lune* a little slower than usual.

"I have to go, but I got a question for you."

"I'll walk you to the door."

I put the cover down on the piano and we went toward the door.

"Can you come out?"

I looked in Mr. Lazar's direction to catch his eye.

"I'll be out just a couple of minutes, Mr. Lazar."

"Take your time," Mr. Lazar said with a smile.

Charles and I walked out and stopped outside the door.

"Would you have dinner with me, Agnieszka?"

I had wondered what it was he needed to tell me and was unprepared for the question.

"What would Miss Morgan think?"

"Lydia? Why should she care?"

"She's your girlfriend, isn't she?"

"No, she isn't. We dated, true. I've dated a few women. But I've never had a girlfriend, not if you mean someone I was at least halfway in love with."

"Are you asking me out on a date, then?"

"I guess I am."

"You haven't noticed anything about me?"

"I've noticed many things about you. So many things that they bother me at night."

That remark brought some heat to my cheeks, but it didn't stop my saying what I thought should have been obvious to him.

"Charles, I'm pregnant."

"You don't look pregnant."

He glanced at my belly.

"Well, I do, when I wear a tight t-shirt."

"Are you married?" He sounded disappointed.

"No." I shook my head, blushing.

"I haven't dated a pregnant woman before. Go out with me?" His eyes twinkled as he peeked at my belly again.

"You don't mind? Won't people talk?"

"Let them talk. You were already pregnant when I first met you, right? I liked you then, so why should it be different now? Besides, I'm falling in love with you and I can't seem to help it."

I was amazed. I had suspected he found me attractive, but falling in love with me? That, I could hardly believe, more so because he announced it on the sidewalk of a busy commercial center. Despite the light cool breeze and the bustle as people rushed by, I felt a growing flush on my cheeks.

"Can I think about it?"

"Sure. I'll give you my phone number. Can you call me when you've thought about it? A 'yes' or a 'no,' call me, please."

"I promise."

"I appreciate it. I'm unfortunately not good at uncertainties."

I already knew what I would say, but I needed to talk to Elise Weisz, to ask her if my decision was right. More than that, I was probably seeking Lenny's permission through her.

Mrs. Weisz listened, without a single word, as I told her about Charles Halverson, how we met, and about his weekly visits with coffee and cookies.

"Are you in love with him?" she asked.

"No. I still love Lenny. I'll always love him. But I won't deny that I like Charles."

"I think you should go out with him. He sounds like a good boy, well-educated and ambitious. But considerate. That's important. This was bound to happen sooner or later. You can't cling to Lenny or your memory of him forever. You have to make a life for yourself."

"I used to think I couldn't after he left the first time. But we had that wonderful weekend. I saw that he did love me and still loved me. He said he left because he really cared for me. I believe him. I know we'd never be together again, but he made it easy for me to look ahead."

I pressed my palm lightly on my belly and added, "And Lenny will always be with me."

"I'll tell him that. He'll be happy to hear it. So few things make him smile nowadays."

She paused and gazed at me in that pensive way she had.

"I hope you won't mind if I don't tell him you've met another man. I think he's being brave and magnanimous in wishing that you find someone new. But I know he'll hurt when he learns you have. I want him alive and happy for as long as possible and I'd lie if I have to. When he's ready, write him. He should hear it from you, not me."

"Mrs. Weisz—Elise—I'm just going out on a date. Charles is not the new man in my life. I wish it continued to be Lenny, but ...."

I couldn't hold back the tears that snuck up on me again. Maybe, I also felt some guilt that I was moving on, leaving Lenny behind.

Elise Weisz squeezed my hand in sympathy and pressed her temple to mine.

"I'm truly sorry, my love, for you, for my son. I wish you two could have had a happy ending. This young man, Charles Halverson, sounds like a fine man. And I have a feeling that he'll turn out right for you. Maybe not now. But later. When you allow yourself to be happy again."

*****

After he asked me out, Charles stopped coming to the music store. I guessed he was letting me reach my decision as freely as possible. When I called him and told him my answer was "yes," all he said in his usual even tone was "I'm glad."

I couldn't tell how uncomfortable he felt, dating a woman whose belly seemed to be growing by the minute. I'd been slow to show until my sixth month. After that, I seemed to explode, but Charles never once made a remark about how much I was growing.

He was always so polite and solicitous those first few weeks. He never pressured me to do anything I felt uncomfortable with and never once made a pass at me.

It wasn't until we'd been dating nearly two months when we kissed for the first time. The kiss was almost a surprise. Before that, he used to drop me off at my building and wait until I had entered it. He never once asked to come up to my apartment.

But when he stopped his car outside my apartment that evening, he held my arm as I reached for the door handle. I turned to ask if he had something to say, but before I could, he put his arms around me and he was kissing me. And, I kissed him back.

"I've been wanting so much to kiss you ever since that night at the concert when I watched the tears rolling down your cheeks. I was so intrigued that you seemed not to have noticed them."

I was, to say the least, incredulous at yet another revelation. I was speechless.

"I think I've been in love with you since then, Agnieszka."

I still couldn't find words for this kind man with his pure loyal heart who waited patiently for months until I was ready to hear him speak about his feelings. I grasped his face and kissed him until we were both breathless. He looked dazed when I let him go. I got out while he was still struggling to steady himself.

From then on, I began to fall in love with Charles. I fell head over hills for Lenny when we first met. Maybe, because it was my first time or maybe he had a charisma that could hit hard at first meeting. But with Charles, discovering the wonder of him took some time and continued after we married.

The weeks that followed were happy in a quiet way, not the excited, impatient happiness Lenny and I felt our first months together, but just as heartfelt.

The next time we met after that passionate car kiss, Charles came up to my apartment. All we did that evening was talk. I told him about Lenny and I learned more about him than I ever had in our early awkward days of dating. Charles could talk cleverly about almost anything under the sun, but about himself, he was shy until I asked him specific questions. That was how I learned that his roots were in Iowa, he had three sisters and a brother, and he was the youngest. His parents were in their forties when they had him. He also told me the history he had with women.

"Did you go out much before Lydia Morgan?"

"Not too much, but enough. I went out with several women, at different periods, of course, but none lasted beyond a month."

"A month? You never dated anyone longer than a month?"

"No, my friends called me 'one-month Charlie'."

"That's funny. Didn't you meet anyone you wanted to go out with longer than that?"

"Not really. Studying and writing papers do take up my time, and no girl I've met induced me to spend time away from my books."

"Until you met Lydia."

"Lydia was part of a bet and she was interesting. As strong and determined as a man."

"A bet?"

"Yeah. My friends made a bet among themselves. The winner is anyone who could find the girl I'd date longer than a month."

"How'd it go?"

"Not too well. Lydia was the last in a string of women my friends set me up with. Most, I dated only once."

"They set you up?"

"Well, yeah. They had to, for the bet."

"And you went along with it?"

"It took the pressure out of meeting women. They got me a blind date about every two months. They might have done more, but I told them that's all I could do. Grad school is not only time-consuming, it's exhausting."

"How long did it take until Lydia?"

"About two years, I think."

"That long. What made Lydia special?"

"We found much to talk about, and she did make classical music sound fascinating, but I don't think there was much physical attraction between us."

"How long did you go out with Lydia?"

"Three months, I think, until I met you."

"Oh, so someone already won the bet."

"I guess so. They've stopped setting me up."

"You mean, they'd go on if not for Lydia?

"My friends were determined."

"Are you still seeing her?"

"No. Not since the first time I brought you coffee and cookies. Are you jealous?"

"No, of course not."

But I lied. I did feel a little jealous.

"I told her I met someone else I think I've fallen in love with. She shrugged her shoulders and that was it. Anyway, I think she's had an on and off relationship with a guy from high school."

"Why me?"

"I need a certain connection to continue seeing a girl, and I never sensed it until I met you."

"But, why me?"

"Because you cry when you hear sad, haunting music. That tells me a lot about you."

He smiled, arching that eyebrow again. Then, he gathered me in his arms.

"You ask too many questions, Agnieszka."

The month before my baby was due, Charles surprised me again.

"Let's get married."

"Don't joke, Charles. Marriage is a serious thing. We've known each other just a few months."

"I can't agree with you more about marriage. You might think I'm just a romantic, with my head in the clouds, but I love you and I can imagine spending my life with you. I see no reason to wait."

"But I'm not sure I love you enough to marry you."

"I'll make you love me more. Give me a chance and I can do it. I know I can."

"You're that confident."

"I know your heart. Your gentle, generous, loving heart."

"I don't think I'm ready for this. I'm not even nineteen yet."

"I'm twenty-six. Doesn't that sound like a good responsible age for a man to marry?"

What about the child I'm carrying?"

"He or she needs a father. Let it be me."

"He has a father."

"Who can't be one to him."

"I know what you say is true, but it hurts to hear you say it."

I cast my eyes down to hide the tears pooling in my eyes. Charles enclosed me in his arms.

"I'm sorry. It's insensitive of me to say that. I know you still love Lenny. I can't replace him in your heart. But I know you have room for me there, as well."

He was right. I didn't love him as much as I did Lenny, but it was also true that I had not known him as long and as intimately. He was such a caring, sensitive, and gentle creature that, with time, I knew I could love him enough to spend a lifetime with him.

I raised my head and gazed straight into Charles' eyes. "Maybe, you're right. Why wait? You don't mind a bride with a beach-ball belly?"

"Not if it's you and not if you don't mind a groom with a pony tail."

He smiled, his eyes brimming with happiness.

*****

I told Tata I was getting married. The three or four times we met since I left the department store, I never mentioned Charles. He shook his head in disapproval.

"I guess you're lucky this man wants to marry you, carrying another man's child. He's a better man than I am. I could never do that. Do you love him?"

"Yes," I said, thinking a simple answer would lead to less discord. Then, I added, "Would you like to meet him?"

"Maybe later. You're full of surprises, Agnieszka, and I'm having trouble keeping up with them. Give me time. I'll catch up."

"So you can't come to the ceremony?"

"You know my answer to that."

"Mama just recognizes church weddings."

"Among other things."

Charles and I married two weeks later in a civil ceremony. Elise Weisz stood as witness. Mr. Lazar and his wife were the only other people we invited.

"I think it's time you write Lenny that letter," Mrs. Weisz said as she hugged me tight.

"You think he's ready?"

"Maybe, I was wrong not to tell him when you first met Charles. He'd be better prepared for this. Still, I think he'll endure this well enough. He wants you to be happy. He's said so, many times. It's me who didn't see things too clearly. He has matured—grown old, in fact—since he was diagnosed and I've refused to admit it. I guess I hoped he would continue to be my young, carefree, smart-mouth son."

She cried quietly on my shoulders. My heart went out to her again for all she had to endure, and I had to steel myself not to cry with her. We clung to each other until we were both calm.

Charles stood patiently by. He seemed to understand what Mrs. Weisz was going through.

"I'm so sorry. I didn't mean to cry like that. Sometimes, I get overwhelmed. I hope I didn't spoil your wedding day."

She dried her tears with some tissues she pulled out of her bag.

"Agnieszka told me you're like a mother to her. Mothers do cry at their daughter's wedding." Charles smiled reassuringly at Elise Weisz.

She returned his smile with her grateful one. "Yes, she's the daughter I never had and you're my new son-in-law. I know Agnieszka made the right choice."

We kept our friendship alive with Mrs. Weisz. When Peter was born, she visited me at the apartment Charles and I moved to. She taught me how to care for my baby, and she doted on him like any grandmother. But for us, a poignant sadness was never far behind.

"Do you realize that I may never have had a grandchild, if it were not for Peter? Robbie could have the gene, too."

"Oh, I'm so sorry, Elise."

"Like Lenny, I was apprehensive when you decided to keep the baby. Now, I believe that if you have him for as long as I have Lenny, you'll be blessed enough."

"I find that reassuring."

Other than my last remark, I didn't give any more thought to that conversation. So absorbed was I in being a new mother and having a part of Lenny for the future. But a month later, a letter from Lenny showed me even more how important Peter was to me.

The letter about my marriage—the last one I wrote Lenny—induced him to write me back. It was the only letter he sent me since we parted and in it, he asked me to stop writing to him so I could focus on my new life. He also said:

I'm not asking you to forget me. I would be telling a lie. I want you to remember me and I'm glad I've left you a lasting memento of me. But I'm truly happy that you're moving on. I wish you well.

Lenny sounded so kind and thoughtful in his letter that it nearly made me cry. But I sensed great hurt behind those wishes for my happiness. He was struggling to deal with loss, lamenting what he could have been and what he and I could have had together. I realized that he was hurting so much that he wanted to put an end to the pain by cutting his ties to me.

I never expected to lose the one way I had to reach Lenny. I hadn't minded that he never wrote me back because his mother kept me up on what was going on with him. But my letters gave me the chance to share with him my intimate thoughts.

He was always happy to receive them, his mother said. So happy that he kept the most recent one on him to read at any time until my next letter. Now, it seemed he needed a clean break from me. That hurt, and I could do nothing about it but remind myself that he was in so much more pain than I was.

If it were not for Peter, I was sure that letter would have depressed me for months. Taking care of him kept me busy. When I held him in my arms, I could feel Lenny's presence.

I remembered Mrs. Weisz's remark and realized that, like me, she saw Lenny in Peter. Maybe, she thought Peter was a reincarnation of her son.

With my baby, Charles's boundless devotion, and Elise Weisz's affection—the kind I wished my mother showed me—I passed a peaceful, happy year. I was lucky, and I knew it.

XIX. Epilogue

The Present ...

Agnieszka Halverson's gaze swept across the faces
of her family. They had listened to her long story
patiently, and their eyes were now glazed but still
focused on her. Goyo had long fallen asleep, snug in his
mother's old bedroom, where his grandfather had put
him to bed. When everyone remained silent, Agnieszka
reached for her glass of water and sipped it slowly for a
few minutes.

It was past two in the morning and still dark
outside. She was exhausted and the cold began to seep
through her sweater. The muscles in her limbs also
quivered a little from having stayed awake past her
usual bedtime. But her heart was light and the pain of
the past tragic week no longer seemed overpowering.

"That's all I can tell you. There isn't much more
that you don't already know. We moved to California a
year later when Charles got a teaching job here, right
after his Ph.D. Peter was one. Justin was born three
years later, Elise, six years after Justin. You all know
what it's been like with your father and me."

She heard Justin clear his throat, loud enough to
call attention on himself. She put her glass back on the
table.

"Would you have told us about your past and Peter's father, if Peter didn't get sick?"

Mrs. Halverson held her son's gaze, disconcerted by his question. It had never occurred to her to ask it of herself.

"I honestly don't know. But, if he had decided to marry or have children, I'm sure I would have. Once he knew, you would, too. There are risks, if he had children, and his wife should know what might be in their future together."

"But don't you think Peter should have known what his future might hold for him, no matter what?"

"I didn't want to worry him. Who knows what the future really holds for us? We plan, act on it, but things can go awry and mess things up. When Peter didn't show signs of illness in his early twenties, like his father did, I hoped he might escape the illness altogether. After that, years went by, good uneventful years."

"But what about the inheritance from his father?"

Dr. Halverson exchanged glances with his wife. He took her hand, enclosed it in his, and answered his son.

"Elise Weisz agreed to put it in a trust. Funds would be released for Peter's care, in case he got sick. Otherwise, it will go to charity. I'm afraid I was the one who insisted on that. For all intents and purposes, Peter was my son from the day he was born. We intended to treat him the same way we did all our children. If he stood out among you, it would have to be for something he did rather than anything special we did for him."

Justin said, "But Peter is special from birth, in his own unique way."

Dr. Halverson caught the irony in Justin's remark.

"You're all unique and special. But, yes, Peter is extra special. Tragically." His voice cracked and he swiped a tear from his eyes.

"Maybe, we should have told Peter, as you suggested, but what if he never got sick? We—your mother, especially—wanted you, our children, to have the best chances for happy lives, like we've had. To that end, we made decisions. Some could no longer be undone. All we can do is live with them."

Justin said no more, but Elise needed more answers.

"You've never told us what happened to your parents, Mom, and I've always wondered why."

"I never saw my mother again after the night I told her and Tata I was pregnant. She passed away less than five years after I got married, before she could forgive me for the bad thing she thought I'd done. My father followed her a few years later. He did visit me at the hospital when Peter was born. I wrote to him a few times after we got here."

"I used to envy my friends who had grandparents because I never met mine. I took it for granted they all had passed away. But now, I see that as sad as I was about it, I find your estrangement with your mother so much sadder."

"Yes. I could have tried to reconcile with her before we came to California. But the truth is I was so caught up making a life for myself and my family to

bother with much else. There was so much I had to
learn."

"What about Dad's parents?"

"They came once to California, from Iowa, when
Justin was two. You weren't born yet. They both
passed away ten years later."

Greg said, "Goyo is lucky that way. He has you
two."

"I'm happy you think so. It used to make me regret
that my children never knew their grandparents."

Agnieszka Halverson smiled broadly at her son-in-
law. She had always liked him very much. He stayed
away from Elise for two years, but she knew he would
seek her out again.

She stood up unsteadily, pulling her husband up
with her.

"If you've got more burning questions, save them
for another day. I'm tired. You all look tired. You're
staying, aren't you, Justin? Too late to return to the
city. Turn all the lights out and lock up when Greg and
your sister leave."

She turned her weary gaze toward Greg and Elise.

"You could leave Goyo here for the night. It's been
a while since he's stayed with us."

"Some other time, Mom. You'll need to rest
tomorrow, and this boy can be a handful."

Agnieszka nodded. With her husband in tow, she
walked straight toward their bedroom. She had laid
bare not only her life, but also her soul to her children.
Now, they would have to deal with everything she told
them.

Whether her story changed how they saw her or not, she was sure of their compassion. It was written on their faces. Elise's, especially. At that, she glowed with pleasure. She had always been unsure how her daughter regarded her. But tonight, she needn't worry. She would sleep better than she did the past week.

In their bedroom, Dr. Halverson said, "Do you regret marrying me?"

"How can you ask me that? I admit it was easier for me to say "yes" when you asked me to marry you thirty-some years ago. I was pregnant and like you, I believed my child was better off having a father. But if I had doubted that I could love you, I wouldn't have married you. Now, let me ask you—did you marry me to rescue me from the shame of being an unwed mother?"

"No, of course not. I had never seen anyone cry, listening to music. That image haunted me for so many nights—you with tears streaming down your cheeks, the look in your eyes when you turned to see if I noticed. It's still floating somewhere in my brain, and every once in a while, it pops up to make me smile."

"I've always believed I've been lucky to have you. You've been good for me and to me. How could I not love you?"

Agnieszka snuggled into his arms.

"I love you, too. Never forget that."

"We've had a good life, you and I. And though Peter is sick, I know I've been more fortunate than Elise Weisz."

*****

"I'm amazed at Mom. I never knew what she had gone through with her parents, how resilient and brave she has been. And Lenny, who would have thought? I always assumed Dad was the love of her life. Do you suppose she still loves Lenny?"

Elise and Greg were in the car on their way home. She was still mulling, with wonder, over everything she heard that evening.

"She could. It's been known to happen—loving two men, or two women equally."

"Mom has such a big heart and so much to give. I can't do that. I'll find it exhausting. I can love only one man so fully."

"Do you think her a better person than you because of that?"

"More generous, for sure. We've chosen different paths, but I've also been luckier because I have her for my mother."

"Yes. It's remarkable she's such a good mother because she didn't have one to model herself after."

"I'm ashamed to admit I took her for granted and didn't feel like I could really get close to her because I couldn't talk to her like I did my Dad. I thought she had no interest in anything but piano and being a good mother. In fact, she's clever, strong, self-assured."

"Like you."

"Yes, but I had better opportunities. Better examples. Dad's pretty remarkable, too. Probably as kind and generous. Me? I don't think I can bear it if you love another in addition to me. But he took Mom on those terms."

"You have no worry with me, my sweet. I'm like your dad. It wasn't until I met you that I fell in love."

"Can you imagine? I might have had a different father if Lenny hadn't been sick. Or, I might not have been born at all."

"My great loss, if that happened."

"You'd have been a bachelor all your life, flitting from flower to flower. Or, married Lori."

"Either way, I would not have known true happiness."

"You're determined to flatter me."

"Not flattery, my love. Truth."

"But how would you know, if I was never born and you never knew me?"

"Because I know myself."

"I shudder to think I might not have been born."

"I'm lucky your Mom and Dad met at the concert hall."

"Mom would have been an unwed mother, like I was. I'm sure being a single mother took more courage in those days."

"More courage than you needed?"

"There's much less stigma about being an unwed mother now. I had Goyo when many single professional women have been raising children on their own without a father. Not so in Mom's generation. Women's lib was just gathering steam then."

"Yes. Agnieszka Halverson has spunk."

"Besides, you came back to me."

"Best thing I ever did. That you still loved me after I kept away so long is a wonder I'll always be grateful for."

"You're my first love."

"And you, mine. We're fated to be together, my love, I'm sure of it."

"As are my parents. Yes, there must be something to fate."

"Did I hear you right? You? Believe in fate? What happened to reason and the power of man to shape his destiny?"

*****

The following day, Elise called her mother, "Mom, did you get a good night sleep after that long ordeal?"

"It wasn't an ordeal. It was a relief. I realized all these years that I've been putting on this façade. I wanted you to have childhoods full of warm happy memories, unlike the one I had; so, I tried to become your typical, doting mother. But I lost myself in the process."

"Mom, you've succeeded very well at being a wonderful mother. But don't you think you're stronger from all you went through earlier?"

"You think so?"

"I know so. You've been through trials I've never had. I'll always be in awe of how well you handled them. I admire you and love you so much and I'm sorry I was an ass to you when I was younger."

"You were headstrong, defiant and, many times, irritating."

"I know. I could have been nicer."

"Believe it or not, you're the daughter I wanted. It may not be obvious, but I think my Mama lives in you. In your choice to defend those who can't afford lawyers, instead of the rich."

"I'm lucky to have you. You and I have something special."

"Thank you. I was never able to say things like that to Mama. So much got in the way. Her morality, I think, was the worst of it."

"Yes, I saw that. I could understand where she was at, given her history, but to cast a daughter aside to satisfy her principles—that, to me, is puzzling."

"I can see I've taught you well."

"You have. You've also taught me to be more accepting of my mistakes, misjudgments. I do try to correct them and hope it's not too late."

"Hindsight is sometimes all you're allowed, and mistakes can drive a point home."

"Can I ask you something and will you tell me the truth?"

"Go ahead."

"Do you still think about Lenny? Do you still love him?"

For a few seconds, there was silence and hesitation at her mother's end.

"Does it matter now? Why do you have to know?"

"I don't have to, but you know how someone else's experience reflects on our own? Greg disappeared on me for a while and I couldn't forget him. I doubted I could fall in love with someone else."

"Do you know Greg reminded me of Lenny? Well, Greg is at least half a foot taller, but Lenny had a similar build in a smaller frame and the same dark brown hair with gold highlights. And your Greg is handsomer."

"Yes, my Greg is beautiful. He seduced you from the very beginning. I saw that. Was it because he bore a resemblance to Lenny? I used to feel that you were pushing us together."

"Well, maybe, I was. But things have turned out quite well for you, haven't they? How many people can have a first love like yours? Strong and true. How many spend their lives with that first love? You've been given a gift, my child. Treasure it."

"We do treasure it more now—Greg and I—after hearing your story."

"I'm glad. Listen, Elise, let's talk some more. I have to go. Your father will be home in an hour. I have this elaborate meal I planned for this evening. I was crazy enough to tell him about it. He'll be expecting it."

"Tell him you changed your plans. He won't mind."

"You're right. He won't. But I'm eager to try these two new dishes. Dad already cut up the vegetables for them a couple of days ago and the meat has been marinating in the refrigerator. I planned it for last night. Why don't you all come for dinner?"

Elise smiled. To her mother, cooking wasn't merely an art; it was also therapy. If she still needed to unwind, an elaborate meal would do it.

"I'd love to, but we need to catch up on sleep."

"I know. Us, too. Well, I'll have to freeze the leftovers for when you come next time. Do I need to remind you Peter is coming home this Friday?"

"I remember. We'll be there."

"Good. Love you. Bye."

*****

Elise picked her son up from his chair, shortly after they finished an early dinner of soup and sandwiches.

"Mommy's tired tonight, sweetheart. Daddy's putting you to bed. After you brush your teeth, of course"

"But I want you to come, say good night to me." Goyo clung tight to his mother's neck.

Elise planted kisses all over her son's face.

"That's what I'm doing now. I'll come after I shower, but you may be asleep. I'll kiss you, anyway. Are you okay with that?"

Goyo nodded, kissing his mother's lips. He yawned and laid his head on his mother's shoulders.

"Come on, kid. We'll brush our teeth together." Greg gently pulled Goyo away from his mother's arms.

He pressed his lips to his wife's ear and gave it a little nibble.

"Can you stay awake long enough to say goodnight to Daddy? Goyo's tired, too, so it shouldn't take me long to tuck him in bed."

"I'm putting the dishes in the dishwasher and taking a shower. I'm afraid I might be too tired and sleepy to promise anything."

"But I have a better prescription for deep, restful sleep."

Sometime later, Elise stood in front of the bathroom mirror, blow-drying her hair. She put the hair dryer down and threaded her fingers through her slightly damp hair. She brushed her hair, separated it into three thick locks, and wove them into a braid. She heard the doorknob turn.

"Leave it loose," Greg said, as he walked into the room.

She watched his reflection on the mirror as he came up to her and encircled her waist with his arms. He playfully tugged at a braided lock of her hair with his teeth and pulled at it.

"Beast," Elise hissed, but she released the thick braid and shook her head until the strands fell loose on her shoulders.

"Much better. You smell so good."

"It's soap, beast. And shampoo."

"No. More than that. You're definitely there."

He nudged her neck and buried his face in her hair. He grabbed the top of her gown with his teeth and pulled it down her shoulders.

"You're being naughty this evening."

"You love naughty. Anyway, I was getting impatient waiting for you to come out of the shower."

"You got impatient in a quarter of an hour?"

"More like a half hour. I should have gone into the shower with you."

"Why didn't you? You could have scrubbed my back."

"I was listening to Goyo's breathing. He's rasping a little."

"Relax already. It's just a cold. And not his first one."

"You're right."

"Is the little beast asleep?"

"As only the innocent can."

"That was quick. Now, you can tuck me in."

"Avec plaisir, madame."

Elise spun around, wound her arms around Greg's neck, pulled his face down to hers, and kissed him. She slithered her hand across his chest down to his stomach, grasped his hand, and led him out of the bathroom.

"First, let's go look in on Goyo. I promised I would."

"Beasts are helpless before imperious Goddesses," Greg sighed and followed.

In Goyo's bedroom, Elise bent over to kiss her son's cheek and briefly placed her ear to his chest.

"He sounds nice, regular, and clear. He has a head cold, and he's breathing through his mouth."

"Good. We can all sleep well tonight."

Later, Elise sat on her side of the bed, Greg on the other. She yawned as he patted her pillows down.

"I talked to Mom this afternoon. I asked her about Lenny."

"Did you find out what you're dying to know?"

"No, she evaded the question and I didn't realize it until much later. Mom could be sly, when she chooses to be. How could I not have seen it before?"

Greg lifted the bed sheet and Elise lay on the bed. He pulled the sheet up and covered her up to her neck.

"Give it up. I don't think she'll ever tell you."

"I'm afraid you're right. She intends to keep it her secret, but you know what I think?"

"I agree with you. Lenny's still in there, somewhere in her heart. Did you ask her about the sapphires and rubies? She never mentioned what she did with those."

"She still has them, wears the rubies a lot and the sapphires, occasionally."

"So, she still does have a place in her heart for Lenny and, maybe, some lingering affection for Aunt Jola."

"You're right. Those stones are treasured mementos."

"She could've sold the sapphires long ago, but she never did. Do you know if her Aunt Jola left her all those earrings?"

"I don't think so. It doesn't matter now, anyway. Mom's conscience is at ease. That's what matters."

"Her conscience? What does she have to feel guilty about?"

"You, men. Justin said the same thing. I think she's wondered many times these last two weeks if she brought Peter into this world for her own selfish needs, to keep Lenny alive in her heart. You know, despite the threat of a devastating disease. With Peter now ill, she may be feeling guilty, wondering if she's like her mother and her grandaunt who used her in their rivalry, and placed her at the center of their personal feud."

"I see. Do you think it helped her to tell her story?"

"She had to, to explain Peter's illness. She might have had qualms, because of her guilt, but she saw we understood and accepted her."

"Yes, it's hard accepting something you feel shame or remorse for. But you need it to help you move on. With Peter so seriously ill, we'll all have trying days ahead, and acceptance can go a long way."

"Yeah, for Mom especially. But she's strong, and now she's sure we'd be there for her."

Elise yawned again. "Aren't you coming to bed?"

"Do you want me to?"

"What kind of a question is that, beast? Would a panther ask that of an inviting prey?"

"An inviting prey is highly unlikely. Anyway, you said you're tired and I still have to shower. Can you wait ten minutes?"

"I don't think panthers bathe. Don't they lick themselves clean? Anyway, this prey can't wait much longer."

"Jezebel," Greg said, grinning, as he took off his robe and climbed into bed.

♥♥♥♥♥

If you're curious about Greg and Elise, read the
first book in the series: *Hello, My Love!* (*Between Two
Worlds, Book 1*)

Beyond broad shoulders and heaving bosoms—a
thoughtful woman's romance novel.

It takes love, not just romance, to face reality and
conquer messy feelings.

In this modern-day pastiche of
Jane Austen novels, Elise is a bright,
beautiful law student, focused on a
career and distrustful of men. She
butts heads with Greg, an alpha male
haunted by past relationships. But
unable to deny their feelings, they
spend a night together. A jilted
fiancée exacts revenge and forces
them to face who they are and what they really want.

A delicious romance with a literary slant, spiced
with a twist of whodunit.

****

The woman in Justin's life has an unlikely history.
Read about it in *Welcome Reluctant Stranger
(Between Two Worlds, Book 3).*

A Riveting Tale of Love, Loss, and Finding Your Own Way.

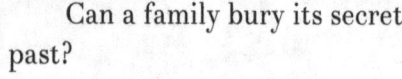

Can a family bury its secret past?

Like her long-lost father, Leilani heals people. But can she heal herself? Accept the awful truth about her father—left behind when her family fled the troubled country of Costa Mora eighteen years ago?

Brokenhearted, Justin just wants to drown his sorrows. But he finds more trouble than he's looking for when thugs assault him and an exotic woman with a dead aim rescues him.

A young woman's inner journey accepting her past spun within a tale of love and past political intrigue.

Read a sequel to Elizabeth Gaskell's *North and South*:

A Victorian feminist tames her man.

What happens after the titillating ending of the BBC miniseries, *North and South*, based on Elizabeth Gaskell's novel?

Gaskell's novel has been described as a romance set against a backdrop of occasionally violent strikes as the working class fought for their rights against tyrannical masters. *Margaret of the North* is a kind of Victorian feminist bildungsroman (coming-of-age novel) couched in romance. The romance is not only in the love between John and Margaret but also in the adventure and excitement that Margaret goes through as she discovers herself and fully realizes her womanhood. It is a journey that happens quietly and mostly internally.

Margaret moves from an idyllic Southern village to a harsh bustling Northern city. There, she confronts her place in a rapidly changing society and her growing awareness of her persona as a woman, one who wants a voice and makes a mark.

ABOUT EJOURNEY

I'm a realist with little imagination—a handicap (or strength) that comes from my training (Ph. D., University of Illinois) and experience as a mental health researcher/evaluator and program developer. I'm also a flâneuse—a female observer-wanderer. So, I watch, observe, listen. And write.

But I'm also a sucker for happy endings. I find enough that depresses me about real life, but seek no catharsis by writing about it. For me, writing is escape, entertainment.

Instead of broad shoulders and heaving bosoms, I explore protagonists' inner conflicts, insecurities, and struggles to grow. Jane Austen and Elizabeth Gaskell inspire me with their awesome feminist heroines.

Author site: http://evyjourney.com

Book blog: http://margaretofthenorth.wordpress.com

Musings on art, travel, food. http://eveonalimb.com

Brief book blurbs: http://sojournerbooks.org

PEACE!

www.ingramcontent.com/pod-product-compliance
Lightning Source LLC
Chambersburg PA
CBHW011441170626
46807CB00009B/3261